I0553344

MIAMI VICES

PAMELA GAIL

Manuscript Prepared By
Brackish Publishing, LLC

Cover Design By
Sweet 15 Designs, LLC

Editing By
Michelle's Edits

To My Friend
Kim Morgan
*You have supported me since this journey started. I appreciate
all your brainstorming, beta reading, ideas and suggestions.
Thank you for always being there for late night conversations
and many laughs.*

ONE
EVAN

Looking around my bare apartment, I'm overwhelmed with the amount of work that still needs to be done. Boxes are stacked against the wall in the living room waiting to be unpacked. Dishes are piled high on the counter and half my clothes are still in suitcases.

I've put off the unpacking process long enough. It needs to get finished today, so I'll be ready for my first day of work. Choosing a box, I open it and start finding a spot for each item as thoughts of the last few months flood my brain.

Moving to Miami was the last thing on my agenda of life goals, yet here I am, starting a new life. I hate the heat, well, Florida in general. It's loud and hot and touristy, not my ideal place to live. Growing up in New Jersey, I prefer the cold. Snow is my favorite thing in the world. Yes, I'm one of those weirdos who loves everything about the harsh winters–shoveling the driveway, building snowmen, hot cocoa, a warm fire, wool sweaters, and fuzzy blankets.

In high school, I worked selling hot dogs to drunk football fans during the Jets and Giants games. The job sucked. Not that I would have enjoyed watching the game. Sports aren't really my thing, but neither is selling hot dogs. Over the years, I moved up and by the time I graduated, I was the assistant manager at one of the concession stands. It wasn't a glamorous job, and the title meant nothing. There were hordes of people over me including my manager and somewhere up the line the people who operate the company that services many of the NFL stadiums across the country.

I never planned to go to college. Truthfully, I had no idea what I wanted to do with my life. When my manager, Nathan, pulled me aside one day and asked if I was interested in becoming a manager for one of the on-site restaurants, I jumped at the idea. It meant more work, but also more money. The catch–I needed a college degree if I wanted to move up higher than managing one restaurant. It took me over a month to decide, but after looking into degrees in hospitality, I decided it might not be so bad. Hospitality gave me other options if I got tired of working at a stadium; plus, I enjoy working with people.

Five years ago, I graduated with my degree. I've been working my way up the ranks since. At first, it pissed me off that I wasn't offered something more after finishing school, but I kept my head down, worked hard, and attempted to save money. The original goal was to buy a home and move out of my parents' house, but my ever-growing credit card debt had different plans. Slowly, I started getting small promotions and opportunities to prove myself.

Football season ended in January since neither team made it past the wild card round, so I took my two weeks' vacation like I always do at the end of the season. Off-season hours are shorter, but there are still concerts and other events that take place during the year, so I don't have six months off like most people think.

April arrived with the first signs of spring. The snow had melted, and the days were warming, but when I arrived the first weekend in April to work at a concert, executives from our parent company, Good Eats, were there. I didn't know who they were at first, then Mavis, my boss, came to the restaurant and asked me to meet her in the conference room. Nerves ate at me as I walked the long hallway to the large room, and I almost passed out when I opened the door and was met with three men in business suits. They introduced themselves and asked me to sit.

Several hours later, I was driving home, my head still spinning. They offered me a job at the Dolphins' stadium in Miami as the Food and Beverage Coordinator. It's a huge promotion and a great opportunity. I'll be in charge of all of the restaurants and bars at the stadium in Florida. The salary is more than double what I was making in New Jersey with more vacation, a 401k, health insurance, and stock options. Maybe the increase in salary will finally enable me to chip away at the massive debt I've accumulated over the past six years. Debt no one knows I have, not even my parents.

I stayed in New Jersey until the middle of July and continued working at my old job. I have to report to the stadium here on August first. Two more days before I'll be thrown into my new position.

When I arrived in Miami two weeks ago, someone from Great Eats met me at the airport and put me up in a hotel until I found an apartment. Once I found an affordable place, they paid for the movers to bring my modest belongings down. I bought a kitchen table and chairs at a used furniture store last week, and my parents gave me a brand-new living room suite complete with a couch, recliner, and coffee table. I need some more storage, but I'm trying not to max out another credit card. Good Eats will pay my rent for the first three months, another benefit of the new job. The experience alone will help with any future opportunity I seek. It was an offer I couldn't pass up.

As my mind wandered, I absently unpacked all the boxes in the living room. It didn't take as long as I expected it would. After breaking down the empty boxes and stacking them near the front door to be taken to the dumpster later, I head for the kitchen. Last week, I unpacked and washed the dishes, but never got around to putting them away. I get the process started, quickly finding a home for everything.

Several times in the past two weeks, I've questioned my decision to take the job. I haven't made any friends in Miami. I miss my home and the folks. I keep telling myself to give it time, but I'm not confident time will make anything better. Moving here was likely a huge mistake. Hell, maybe Mike was right all along. I probably can't do this. Those thoughts—and many more, all negative—race through my mind. I'm questioning every life decision as I unpack the suitcases and put away my clothes. Maybe I should cut my losses and move home before I have the chance to screw up.

TWO
ISAAC

As soon as the water is scalding, I step into the shower and feel the tension drain from my sore muscles. Practice kicked my ass today and I'm grateful for the heat and pounding spray. Not sure what possessed the team's owner to spring for these upscale shower heads, but they beat paying for a masseuse.

Miami has been my home for six years. The Dolphins were not my top choice, but being drafted number one fresh out of high school is an accomplishment few can claim. Don't get me wrong, I'm not complaining about being the number one draft pick at eighteen, but if I'd had a choice, I would have chosen a different team.

Growing up in the northeast, I had many teams to choose from to support, but my dad was born in Mexico and raised in Texas. He's a diehard Texans fan, no matter how they play. I love the Texans because my dad loves the Texans. He always dreamed of going pro, but an injury in college derailed that dream. My brothers and I played football growing up, but I'm the only one who went pro. My older brother, Owen, played in college, but my younger brother, Aiden, quit after middle school. He never loved the game as much as the rest of us.

Practices started about six weeks ago and I'm glad to be back on the field every day. The off-season is difficult for me. I get antsy, waiting to be back in my element and count the days until late May when we can officially start practicing again. I keep up with my workouts and visit family during my time off, but I get bored. Boredom has never been good for me. I get inside my own head and fast food comforts me. I don't have many vices. I rarely drink, and I don't smoke or use drugs, but greasy, crappy fast food does it for me. If my coaches knew how often I eat that shit, they'd have my ass.

Pulling myself back to reality, I turn the shower off and towel dry. My muscles ache from pushing hard and working my ass off at practice. Once I finish, I pull on shorts and a t-shirt. I miss the cold weather in the height of the Miami summer when temperatures reach triple digits, but I'll never miss shoveling snow. I shudder at the thought.

"Yo, Isaac," Tyson Sanders, our quarterback, calls. "You coming out with us tonight?"

Same question every Friday after practice. I'm close to a few of the guys on the team, but I don't go out often. I don't like the bar scene. I've never dated much, and I don't care for casual hookups. I've had them, but I'm looking for more. Right now, I prefer to focus on my career. I'm only twenty-four. There's plenty of time to settle down.

"Nah, I'm beat." It's not a lie. I am exhausted from practice, but I'll likely pick up junk food from a drive thru and stay up for hours binging a few action movies.

It gets lonely, but I'm not good with people. During the season, all eyes are on me constantly. I prefer my privacy, so I work hard not to put myself in a position where my name will end up in the headlines or tabloids. Some of my team-mates don't feel the same way and give zero fucks about their life being on full display for the world. The only things I want people to talk about are my accomplishments on the field.

Tyson shakes his head but doesn't argue or push me. He respects my need for privacy. Tyson is a partier and doesn't care what anyone thinks about him or what is said on social media. He is comfortable with who he is. I admire him for that. He's also my closest friend on the team. As much as he loves to party and hookup with random girls, he'll come hang out with me and watch movies or play video games any time I invite him. Tyson was my mentor when I joined the team, and we became fast friends. If I asked him to come chill tonight, he'd blow off the other guys, but I refuse to put him in that position. It's not his place to babysit me.

He waves as he follows a few other guys out. I grab my black gym bag and head to my car. As soon as my phone connects to Bluetooth, I hit my mom's cell number. I haven't talked to my parents since Sunday. I miss them every day and wish we all lived closer.

"Hey, baby," Mom answers on the second ring. She's never far from her phone, especially now that all her children have moved out.

"Hi, Mom, how are you and Dad?"

"Wonderful. We're enjoying having Aiden here but miss you so much. Owen and the girls are here for the weekend."

She was so excited when my little brother decided to come home for the summer. He'll be a college senior this year at the University of Hartford in Connecticut and plans to move to California after graduation. Honestly, I was shocked when he took a job in our hometown for the summer instead of an internship in California or New York. He is getting a degree in audio engineering and wants to be a sound designer for movies or television. He's a master at sound design and has been working with local bands since high school.

Owen lives in New Jersey about an hour from our parents. He spends at least one weekend a month with them. He works for an insurance company and is able to work from home most of the time. It allows him flexibility to be available for his girls. Raising two daughters alone isn't an easy task, but Owen is a great father. His wife filed for divorce three years ago when their youngest was only six months old. She didn't even try to get custody of the girls. She'll call him a couple of times a year and ask to visit them. Owen never denies her request. I'm not sure I would be so nice after everything she put him through.

"I'm glad your house is full. I miss you guys, too."

"How is Miami? Is practice going well?" she asks.

"Miami is hot. Practice is going great. The team looks good, so we should be more than ready by September."

"That's good news, son," Dad adds, joining Mom on the call. I love that she always puts me on speaker phone, and they all join the conversation.

"Hey, Dad. Hi Aiden and Owen, how's life?"

"Pretty good. Looking forward to senior year," Aiden says.

"Busy, but I wouldn't have it any other way," Owen adds, and I can hear the smile in his voice. He loves being a father more than anything in the world.

"Are my nieces there?"

"Hi, Uncle Isaac," Katie squeals with a giggle.

"Hi," Kennedy whispers. She's the shyest three-year-old I've ever met, but Katie makes up for it by being the loudest five-year-old this side of the Mississippi.

"Hey, baby girls. Uncle Isaac misses you so much."

Talking to my family is always the highlight of my day. I don't speak to them every day, but we do talk several times a week. I continue the conversation with my family for the entire twenty-minute drive to my modest house. I live in a gated community for safety reasons, but I bought a small three-bedroom house. It's just me, so I don't need a lot of room, but I like having extra bedrooms when my family visits. They all try to make it down for at least one game each season. I look forward to seeing them in a couple of months. It sucks not being able to spend much time with my family and missing most of the major holidays, but that's the life of an NFL player and one I refuse to trade it for anything.

THREE
EVAN

 As I drive through the security gate and into the employee parking lot, nerves eat at me. I spent the first twenty-seven years of my life living in the same house with my parents. I didn't even leave town for school, attending the local college. Here I am, starting a new life more than thirteen hundred miles from the only home I've ever known. The past two weeks felt more like a vacation than a real move. Today, that changes. Now, it's real. This is my new life. The feeling of sheer loneliness washes over me. It's been building for a few days. The longer I'm in Miami the more relaxed I should feel, but instead, I feel more and more lonely and out of place.

Pulling into the first space I find, I check to make sure I have my keys, wallet, and phone. I'm infamous for leaving crap behind. After gathering strength I don't feel, I get out of the car, locking it behind me and heading for the employee entrance. My predecessor will be here for the next week, training me before she leaves for her new job somewhere on the west coast.

I hit the buzzer and wait to be let inside. I double check the instructions on my phone. A loud buzz sounds then a click indicating the door is unlocked. Tentatively, I open the door then take the hallway to the left and start reading door numbers. When I get to 108, the door is open and a petite woman with graying hair is sitting behind the desk closest to the door.

"Good morning, you must be Mr. Nichols," she says with a bright smile, offering me her hand.

Shaking it, I respond, "Yes, but please call me Evan."

"It's nice to meet you, Evan. I'm Hope Masters, Sandy Covington's assistant and soon to be your assistant."

"It's great to meet you, too. Do you prefer Ms. Masters or Hope?"

"Hope, please. Most of us go by our first names around here."

"Excellent," I agree. I prefer first names. Using last names seems too formal and that is not my style.

"Let me show you around. For now, this will be your desk," she starts, pointing to a large desk by the window already set up with a laptop. "Here is a packet of information Sandy and I put together for you. It has all your basic information, including passwords and how to change them so you can get into your computer, the food service sites, and other pertinent information. Feel free to read through it at your leisure. Sandy and I will be going through everything in the folder over the next week but thought it would be nice to have it printed as well."

"Yes, thank you. I'm sure I'll be referencing this folder for a few months until I get the lay of the land."

Taking out a set of keys, she opens the door on the opposite side of the room and leads me inside. "This is the conference room where we hold our monthly food service meetings.

The next one is on the fourth. Sandy will help prepare for that meeting and lead it with you. Beginning in September, you will lead those meetings, but don't worry, I'll be here if you have any questions." Locking the door behind us, she leads me to the other side of the large office and knocks on the door.

"Come in," a voice calls from the other side.

"Sandy likes to leave her door closed, but you can decide if you prefer it opened or closed once you move into the office," she explains, leading me inside.

I will likely leave it open unless I'm in a meeting or on a call and can't be disturbed. I can't imagine closing myself off from everyone else.

"Sandy, this is Evan Nichols, I was just showing him around. Would you like to join us for the tour?"

"Evan, it is so nice to meet you," she says, shaking my hand.

"Nice to meet you as well."

"I think I'll wait here and get a few things ready for Evan while you take him on the grand tour. Evan, when you return, join me in the conference room and we'll go over some paperwork and then get started with training."

"Sounds good to me," I agree.

"Shall we?" Hope offers, gesturing for me to follow her. We spend the next hour walking through the stadium. She shows me the employee kitchen, which is huge and fully stocked with snacks and beverages. Then she takes me to each restaurant, bar, concession stand, and cart. Before the tour ends, we take a look at the field from the employee box. It's an impressive view.

"You are allowed to access the box during any game or concert. As the coordinator, most of your work is done Monday through Friday from 8-5, but you will need to be available during the home games in case an emergency arises. This is the perfect place to enjoy the game unless you're needed."

"Do all the employees have access to this box?"

"Just the managers, directors, and their assistants on a regular basis. Most of the other employees are actually working during the games. However, we do encourage employees to choose a game, concert, or event during the year and request it off, so they have the opportunity to enjoy the box once a year. Some take us up on the offer, but many don't."

"That's a nice perk."

"Was that not an option at your former stadium?"

"No. Not at my level at least." Honestly, I'm not sure we had an employee box, but I don't share that with Hope.

"I guess every stadium is different." She shrugs as she leads me out of the box and to the elevator. We take it to ground level and I follow her through the tunnels past the Dolphins locker room and onto the field. We stay on the side-lines and watch practice for a few minutes."

"Wow! This is amazing. I never went on the field in New Jersey."

"You have to see it. The view from the box is breathtaking, but nothing compares to being on the field."

"You sound like you really like football."

"Are you kidding me? I never miss a home game. I grew up here and have been a huge Dolphins fan my entire life. My father was the general manager of the team for twenty years. When I turned sixteen, I applied for a job here. I started as an usher and moved to various positions over the years until I landed my current position—Assistant to the Food and Beverage Coordinator. I've been in this position for twenty-five years and you'll be the third coordinator I've worked for. I love my job and this stadium. My youngest son is a free agent and was just hired as the backup quarterback. It's good to have him home. He's played for three other NFL teams and as much as he's enjoyed his career, his dream was to eventually make his way onto the Dolphins' roster." Hope beams with pride and I see nothing but love for this team and city in her eyes.

"That's great, Hope. I can tell you're very proud of him."

"I am. My other son is a reporter for the team and my daughters both work in the Dolphins' marketing department."

"You have your whole family here."

"Except my husband. He's an ER nurse."

"Hey, Momma," a handsome man who looks to be in his early thirties jogs over to us.

"Hi, Carter. How's my baby boy?"

"Not so much a baby," he winks.

"This is Evan. He's taking Sandy's position. This is my son, Carter."

We exchange handshakes and greetings before he jogs back onto the field to join his teammates. As we turn to go back through the tunnel, I run smack into a wall of muscles.

"Eh, ex-excuse me," I stutter, taking a step back and almost losing my balance. He grabs my arm to steady me and warmth shoots through me. Damn, he's gorgeous with his olive skin, dark eyes, and short, brown hair. I shake my head in an effort to focus and realize he said something that didn't register.

"I'm sorry. What did you say?"

"Are you okay? I didn't see you when I came around the corner."

"I'm fine."

He nods quickly and I swear he licks his lips as his gaze looks me over from head to toe. Then he focuses on my eyes.

"Have a good day." He winks before jogging through the tunnel toward the field.

When I look at Hope, she has a hint of humor in her eyes and a huge smile on her face.

"Who was that?" I ask.

"Isaac Flores, wide receiver."

"That's Isaac Flores? He's not just any wide receiver. He was drafted straight out of high school. He's the best in the NFL."

"You know football."

"Yeah, not so much. I wasn't much of a fan before I started working at the stadium in New Jersey. That first year, I had a manager who was a huge fan and could spit out any stat or fact from the past fifty years. Her enthusiasm was definitely contagious. We started watching games together when we weren't working and now, I follow several teams including the Giants and Jets. I'm not great at remembering stats, but I know a few key players."

"I can see those being teams you follow. Sometimes, it's about proximity. My dad's the reason I love the Dolphins. I guess I'm the reason my kids love the team."

"That makes sense."

After a stop at the HR office to get my photo taken for my badge, Hope leads me back to the office, where Sandy is waiting with papers spread across the conference room table. After completing paperwork, Sandy gives me a map of the stadium to add to my folder, then we spend a few hours going over the information Hope gave me when I first arrived.

By the time five rolls around, my new badge has been delivered, so I can access the building anytime. Even though I'm mentally exhausted, I try to take my folder and laptop home to do some reading and to learn more about the new job, but Sandy insists that I take a break for tonight. She's right. I need to let my brain rest. For me, that's not always a good thing. A resting brain only allows me time to think about all the shit I can cause to go wrong in the next few weeks.

FOUR
ISAAC

Practice was brutal today, but it always is this time of year. We have less than six weeks before our season opener, and we have a lot of work to do. By the time I make it home, my muscles are screaming. I toss my keys into the bowl by the front door and grab a bottle of water from the fridge before connecting my tablet to the surround sound and blasting my favorite boy-band playlist through the entire house. Backstreet Boys fills the room. I drop onto the couch and open the greasy bag, pulling out three burgers, two large fries and an apple pie. This is the perfect end to a long day. My favorite music, greasy fast food, and the most comfortable couch I've ever sat on. I'll be lucky to make it past eight o'clock before passing out from sheer exhaustion.

While I tear through my burgers, visions of a sexy smile flash in my head as I think about the man I almost clobbered today—tall and lean with short, brown hair, perfectly-trimmed facial hair, brown eyes, absolutely gorgeous. He was dressed to impress in khaki pants and a blue polo that looked amazing against his pale skin. I haven't been able to get him out of my mind. He invaded my thoughts during practice, in the shower, while Coach gave us his after-practice lecture, driving home, and now as I eat dinner. I have to find out who he is. I hope he is a new employee, and I will run into him again. I'd ask Carter Masters since the guy was with his mom, but Carter doesn't know I'm gay. No one knows and I'd like to keep it that way.

Meeting guys is almost impossible as one of the most well-known NFL players in the country. I do my best to keep a low profile. I rarely go out and haven't dated in years. I have no desire for my private life to be blasted all over the internet and that's exactly what will happen if my secret gets out. There has to be a way for me to figure out who this guy is and still keep my personal life private.

I try to keep thoughts of that gorgeous man out of my head as I clean up my mess, take the trash out and wash the dishes I left in the sink this morning. Instead of returning to the couch, I drag myself down the hallway to the master suite. If I sit back on the couch, I'll wake up there in the morning and that's the last thing my body needs. My frame is much too big to stretch out on the couch and I always regret it when I fall asleep there.

My phone dings with a text as I get comfortable on my California king bed.

> Tyson: Come out with us. Heading to South
> Beach to hit some clubs.

I consider ignoring his text, but if I do, I'll catch hell tomorrow. Who am I kidding? I'm going to catch hell when I turn him down again. I'm all for a good party, but not during the season when practice is kicking my ass.

> Me: Not tonight. I'm already kicked up with some trash TV.

It's not really a lie. I haven't actually landed on a show, but I'm scrolling through my options.

> Tyson: Come on, Old Man. You're the baby of the team, but act like my grandpa.

> Tyson: Actually, I think my grandpa parties more than you.

Tyson is always teasing me about being old. In fact, he coined the nickname 'Old Man' about two years ago and it stuck. If it wasn't so damn true, it might piss me off.

> Me: Guilt me all you want. It's not going to work.

> Me: Call grandpa. He can take my place.

Tyson responds with a bunch of laughing emojis before letting me off the hook with a final text.

> Tyson: Fine. Next time, you're joining us. You gotta come out at least once before our first game.

> Me: Deal.

I agree because he's right. I enjoy hanging out with the team, but I won't do it once the games start. If I don't go out with them soon, it will be February before I let them drag me to a club.

I silence my phone and put it on the charger for the night. Nothing caught my attention, so I click off the TV since and turn off the lights with the remote next to my bed. No use staying awake. I might as well get some sleep. Tomorrow is going to be another long day of conditioning and practice and I absolutely love every second of it.

EVAN

 Much to Hope's disappointment, I did not leave work at five or six or even seven. She finally called it a night at six-thirty when I insisted she leave. She's been doing her job for years and knows exactly what to do and when. I still have a lot to learn and there is no reason for her to stay late just because I do. I appreciate her willingness to go the extra mile, but I don't expect my employees to work overtime hours unless it's absolutely necessary and if that happens, I will make sure they get compensated. I've never understood bosses who expect their employees to work for free. I've been fortunate that I haven't experienced that so far in my career. I've had some great bosses over the years. Now that I'm the boss, I want to be like the good ones I've had.

It's almost eight when I finally reach my car after shutting everything down and locking up. Hopefully, I'll start to get the hang of the job in the next few weeks, so I can cut back on some of the extended hours. Being a salaried employee, I don't get the benefit of overtime and even if it was an option,

I would refuse. I don't believe I should be paid for choosing to stay late and learn more about my job.

I'm pulling out onto the highway when my phone rings. There's more traffic than I expected, so I don't bother looking at the number before I hit the connect button on the side of my steering wheel. It's probably my parents. I haven't spoken to them in five days, the longest I've ever gone without at least one conversation.

"Hello," I say as I merge onto the expressway and almost immediately come to a complete stop. Must be an accident or road construction. I'm still not familiar with the city, so I don't know an alternate route to my apartment.

"Evan," the deep voice on the other end of the phone replies and my heart sinks. "Have you fucked up the new job and come crawling back to mommy and daddy yet?"

My heart stops. I can't breathe. Thank goodness I'm stopped, or I might have wrecked the car when he spoke.

"The job is good," I finally find words to respond. Mike was my boyfriend until I moved to Miami. We broke up, which was the best part of taking this job, and we haven't spoken since a few days before I left Rutherford.

"Doubtful," he scoffs. "You know as well as I do that you're going to fail miserably with this venture. It's in your blood. You can't help but be a complete and utter fuck up at everything in your life. Come on, Evvy," he continues in his typical condescending voice. "You know you're in over your head. It's time to give up before you dig yourself into a hole you can't climb out of."

I hate when he calls me Evvy. What kind of name is that? It certainly isn't short for Evan.

"Is there something you need?" I snap. I'm not in the mood for Mike tonight. He's an ass and I allowed him to rule my life for far too long. The more he talks, the more my heart races, and my hands shake. If traffic wasn't at a standstill, I'd be pulling over.

"For starters, you need to stop playing this game and come home where you belong. You will never be able to make it without me." Is he serious? I can do this without him. I think. "I know what you're thinking. You're questioning your decision because you know I'm right."

"I'm doing fine here," I squeak out, giving away the fact that he's getting to me.

"Are you really, Evvy? It's time to give up. I'll get you a job here, so you can actually make a decent living. You will move in with me and take care of my home and me. I'll even allow you to choose the meals you cook at least twice a week. You're shit at planning menus, but at least you're a decent cook."

"So, you want me to quit my job, move in with you, and be your chef?"

"Not at all. You will be in charge of cooking, cleaning, taking care of the house and yard, but you will also need to get a job. I expect you to pay your way. I'm not dating some freeloader."

Wow, such a generous bastard. "You're not dating me at all. We broke up," I say with confidence I don't feel.

"Hahaha, that's funny. You pitched your little tantrum and moved away for a month. I allowed it because it was time for you to see how much you actually need me in order to function. But now, I'm sick of this game and expect you to be back in New Jersey and moved into my home by the weekend. That gives you three days. It's not like you have much to move. I mean, can you even afford furniture or are you living on a street corner?"

"I'm not moving back to Jersey and if I ever choose to come back, it sure won't be for you." I disconnect the call before Mike can respond. As I pass the accident and traffic starts moving at a steady pace, the phone rings again. This time, I glance at the screen and see Mike's name. I ignore the call. I'm still shaking from the last encounter. Talking to anyone, especially Mike, that way is not my normal personality. I'm a pushover, which is why I allowed Mike to control me for so long.

It will take time to get settled here and think of Miami as my home, but I like the job and my apartment. For the first time in my life, I'm completely on my own and I'm slowly finding my way. The job is only difficult because it's new. Every day, I feel more confident and like I'm getting the hang of one more thing.

In the twenty minutes it takes me to drive the rest of the way home, Mike calls three more times and I ignore him all three times. I can visualize him fuming while pacing his house. He's always been a pacer when he gets angry, which seemed to be constantly when we were dating.

When I get inside my apartment, I skip the shower, strip down to my underwear, and fall into bed. I should eat dinner, but the conversation with Mike stole my appetite. I'm physically and mentally exhausted, yet sleep doesn't come. I toss and turn for hours, Mike's words playing on repeat.

Work has always come easy for me. At my old job, it was the only part of my life where I had any confidence in my abilities. Starting over broke some of that confidence and some days, I feel like I'm floundering and should have stayed in New Jersey. At twenty-seven, it was time for me to move out on my own and figure out my life.

Crawling back to Mike isn't an option no matter what happens in Miami. Even if I do fail here, he'll never know. He's probably right, though. I'm not good at being alone. I miss my parents and the familiarity of my hometown. Here, all I know is how to get from my apartment to the stadium and the grocery store. It's kind of sad. I should have ventured out more before the job started.

When sunlight begins to peek through the blinds, I groan and pick up my phone. Already close to seven and sleep eluded me most of the night. Today is going to be miserable. I hope I can stay awake. We don't have any concerts this weekend and the season opener is still a couple of weeks away. Maybe I can leave a little early and get some rest. Damn Mike for getting inside my head again. And damn me for allowing it to happen.

SIX

ISAAC

The parking lot at Club Tango is almost full and there is a line for the valet. Instead of waiting in line, I choose to self-park. I don't want to be here, but I promised Tyson and the guys I'd join them one night before the season starts. We have less than two weeks, so it's time to make good on my word. I drove so I'll have an excuse to not drink. As long as I stay sober, I can sneak off when the others get wasted and start pairing off with their random hookups.

After putting the car in park, I lean my head against the back of the seat and close my eyes.

"You can do this. It's one night then you're off the hook until February," I give myself a little pep talk. "Go inside. Pretend to flirt with a few girls then call it a night."

Slowly, I open the car door and climb out, dragging my feet to the door. It's only nine-thirty and the line to get in is around the corner. Thankful for small favors, I pass the line and walk up to the door guy. He sees me coming and moves the velvet rope blocking the VIP entrance. Perks of being a Dolphins' player.

"Hey, man, good to see you," he greets as I pass. I've known Damien for a few years. I don't go out much, but this is always our first stop and often the only one.

"What's up?" I respond with a quick handshake as I pass.

Music blasts from every corner of the large room. The club is mostly dark with neon lights illuminating the dance floor. On the left side is a huge bar that spans the room from one wall to the other. Between the bar and dance floor are a few tables scattered around and private booths line the wall. Upstairs are the VIP suites, several smaller rooms with floor to ceiling windows, so those inside can hear and see what's happening in the club. The walkway outside of the suites wraps around the entire upstairs and the center in open so you can look over the railing onto the dance floor.

I make my way up to our regular suite, the one Tyson has reserved for every Friday night of the year, whether we use it or not. I don't know how much he pays to keep it on reserve, but it's worth it. Once inside the room, it's a little quieter. The room is decked out in high-end leather couches and chairs, a few tables, a bar with personal bartender, and a private bathroom.

When I walk in, I find several guys from the team are here along with some groupies. That might not be the right word, but these are girls who don't care anything about football and probably don't know the difference between a football and a baseball. They are here for the money and status. They don't come to any games, but they always find their way to Club Tango on Friday night and end up in our suite. Tyson talks shit about a few of them even though he's hooked up with most of them and currently has a scantily dressed girl on each arm. He's smiling and laughing, laying on the charm.

"No, shit, you did show up." Tyson lets go of the girls when he spots me, making his way over. He claps me on the back. "What are you drinking?"

"Water. I'm driving."

"You're driving? Why didn't you call for a car?"

"Yeah, Old Man," Carter adds, joining our conversation. "You can't come to the land of plenty," he continues, spreading his arms to indicate all the girls around the room, "and not have a few drinks. Come on, it will loosen you up then maybe we can get you laid for once."

"I do fine on my own," I growl.

"Yeah, but your hand must be getting tired." I glare at Carter, the little asshole, ready to make some asinine comment back, but Tyson steps in.

"Enough, Carter. Give the boy a break." At Tyson's words, Carter shrugs and steps away, following a girl in a short, pink skirt, and I mean *short*. I can see her ass cheeks hanging out the bottom and she is definitely not wearing underwear.

By the time I face Tyson, Carter already has an arm wrapped around Pink Skirt. "I'm not in the mood for this shit tonight."

"I get it, but thanks for gracing us with your presence, oh mighty Old Man."

"Bitch."

Tyson laughs. "Come on, let's get you something resembling a drink, so no one gives you shit for the rest of the week."

"Or season."

"You're probably right about that."

I follow Tyson to the bar, and he orders himself a beer and a shot of tequila and me a club soda with a lime. Tyson is the only one on the team who knows I'm gay. He talks to me about girls and pretends he's always trying to get me laid in an effort to keep my secret. I tried to keep it from him, but I was struggling with my sexuality and being new to the team at such a young age. Tyson took me out to dinner one day a couple of weeks after practice started to make sure I was doing alright. I confided in him that night that I was struggling being on my own for the first time and I was a little homesick. He didn't make fun of me or tell anyone else. Over the next few months, we built a strong friendship, and I started trusting him. Eventually, I told him the truth. He supported me and told me he'd keep my secret. For the past six years, he's made good on that promise.

"Here you go." Tyson hands me my drink then downs his shot of tequila before picking up his beer and motioning for me to follow him. He leads me to a small table with two chairs away from everyone else. The table is in the corner near the bathroom and rarely gets used. I don't come often, but it's basically the same night with most of the same girls every time I'm here. These boys need to branch out a little.

We sit in silence for a few minutes, while Tyson sips his beer and I watch the crowd gathering in the room. More guys from the team show up and a few have girls with them.

"I know this isn't your scene, but I'm glad you're here," Tyson breaks the silence.

"Yeah," is all I manage to say. How do I respond to him? He's right, this isn't my scene. The loud techno and dance music, the drunk girls, having to hide who I am – sometimes it's all too much. It's the reason I don't like to come out. Keeping my secret is easier when I stick to playing football and going home.

"Loosen up. You'll be fine."

I turn my head to stare at Tyson, "I'm not up for fake flirting and having girls all over me."

"They won't bite," he teases. "Well, some of them do, but I like it." Tyson winks.

"Gross."

"Really? You find *that* gross?"

"Okay," I hold my hands up in surrender. "You probably find what I do gross, too."

"Actually, I don't think about what you do."

"Good point. I normally don't think about what you do, either."

We clink our glasses and I take a sip of my club soda. It's not very good, but at least it looks like a vodka soda or gin and tonic. No one is going to question me. As I sip my drink slowly, making it last as long as possible, I watch my teammates. Some are already making out with girls, others are going shot for shot at the bar, and a few are in smaller groups, talking and laughing. If I wasn't so wound up, it might be fun.

Mark Sharkey, our tight end, saunters over with two girls. He pulls up three more chairs and offers one to each girl before dropping into the third one.

"This is Tawny and Crystal," he introduces us. "That's Tyson and that's Isaac." He points to each of us as he speaks.

The brunette is sitting closest to me and leans in, "Nice to meet you, Isaac," she purrs, running a hand up my leg. My whole body goes rigid. I scoot my chair back a little, turning it toward the table, causing her hand to fall. She gives a dirty look then sits back in the chair and turns her attention to Mark, who is looking at me like I've lost my mind.

"Damn, you really are an old man," he snaps with a shake of his head. "Tawny here's a sure thing. She'll give you a blow job in the bathroom right now. Just say the word."

For a split second, I considered this option. It would get the guys off my back and if I close my eyes, I can imagine it's a man. I mean, a blow job is a blow job.

"Yeah, baby, come on. I already took care of Marky once tonight. I can show you a good time, too."

Those words shatter all thoughts of taking her up on the offer. "No thanks." Getting a blow job in the bathroom right after she gave one to my teammate isn't happening. Disgusting. "I don't want his leftovers," I bark.

Pushing up from the chair, I don't wait for her or Mark to respond. I'm downstairs and almost at the exit when Tyson catches up to me.

"You okay?" he asks, grabbing my arm and stopping me from leaving.

"I'm fine, but I'm not doing this tonight."

"Mark always goes too far."

"That's who he is and that's fine, but I'm not pretending to be interested in any of the girls, and I'm sure as shit not taking one to the bathroom."

"Come on, let's go get a bunch greasy food and watch a movie at my place," he offers.

I take a deep breath and let it out slowly, releasing some of the tension in my body. "Nah, you go get yourself laid. I'm fine."

"You sure?"

"I'm sure."

With a smile, Tyson turns back to the club and rushes up the steps while I walk to my car. It was nice of him to offer to keep me company, but I don't need to be his charity case. I pull out of the parking lot and head in the direction of my favorite drive thru. Tyson is right about one thing; greasy food sounds a little like heaven right now.

SEVEN
EVAN

 Sandy's been gone a few weeks and I'm slowly starting to feel like I'm getting the hang of the job. Hope is a godsend. She knows this job and stadium backwards and forwards. I definitely would have been lost my first few weeks without her. Sandy taught me a lot, but by the end of the week, she had checked out. Hope filled in the gaps Sandy left out.

I've been so busy trying to learn the ropes I haven't taken time to move into Sandy's old office. I guess I can start calling it my office. Hope laughs at me every time I call it Sandy's office. Maybe once I get settled into the space it will start to feel like my office. Saturday should be a relaxing day, but I know if I don't take time on my day off to get set up in my office, I never will.

I'm shocked when I walk in and Hope is there with three Dolphins' players. One I recognize as her son, Carter, one I don't know, and the third is the wall of muscles I ran into on my first day here.

It takes a second for me to catch my breath. Seeing that gorgeous man again has me all kinds of worked up. When I'm able to speak without sounding like a prepubescent boy, I ask, "What's all this?" I motion to the boxes leaned up against the wall closest to the door.

"It was time for an upgrade." Hope shrugs as if this all perfectly reasonable for a Saturday morning. "I put in a request a few weeks ago for new furniture for the office. It got approved, so I wrangled up my son and a couple of his friends to help set everything up. I didn't expect to see you today.

"Well, I figured today was a day to get settled into my office. Great minds and all."

"Perfect timing," she agrees. "I was going to surprise you, but since you're here if there is anything I picked out that you don't like, we can return it and order something you want."

"Hope, it will be perfect. I'm sure I will love everything you chose."

I do my best to focus on Hope and our conversation instead of the gorgeous Isaac Flores. It's not an easy task. My face heats when I fail miserably, and he catches me checking him out. He smiles at me, and I swear he's checking me out, too. I shake my head to focus. *Get it together, Evan.* Isaac likely has women lining up. He isn't interested in someone like me.

Hope makes some quick introductions and I find out the other guy is Tyson Sanders, the quarterback. Immediately after introductions, the guys get busy moving furniture out of my office. Hope has already packed up everything that stays so they have the room empty in no time.

Tyson drags the box with my new desk into the office and gets to work building it with help from Carter. Isaac does the same with the box holding my new bookcase and motions for me to follow him. *Yes!* I try to appear nonchalant as excitement courses through my body. I've been hoping for an introduction to Isaac Flores for the past three weeks. Hell, I would have settled for a simple glimpse, but I've been too busy to find my way back to the employee box or field during practice. I had resigned myself to never seeing him again, yet here he is standing in my office opening a giant box.

We silently get to work building the bookcase. I want to talk to him, but I have no idea what to say. My mind is completely blank as the silence stretches between us bordering on uncomfortable. He is basically building the bookcase while I watch. Nope, this isn't awkward at all.

"Can you hand me the screwdriver?" Isaac asks, pulling me out of my own thoughts.

"Sure," I reach into the toolbox and pull out two. "Flat head or Phillips?"

"Phillips."

I hand him the correct one and toss the other one back into the toolbox.

"Can you hold this steady?"

I do as he asks and hold the board steady while he screws it to the one he's holding.

Tyson and Carter joke and tease each other on the other side of the room and I can't help but laugh at them.

"They're always like this," Isaac whispers. "Worse than two kids."

"You know we can hear you, Old Man," Tyson calls.

Old? I could have sworn Isaac was younger than both of the other guys. Maybe I should have done some online stalking. I thought about it, but I'm too tired to think straight by the time I get home most nights. I know it will get easier once I learn all the ins and outs of the job, but right now, I'm physically and mentally worn out.

"You're almost ten years older than me," Isaac claps back.

"Yeah, but you holed up in your house alone while the rest of us know how to have a good time," Tyson tosses back.

"You act older than my mother," Carter piles on.

"Hey, I'm not old. You better watch your mouth, little boy," Hope teases with a glint of humor in her eyes. Her voice sounds stern, but her smile gives her away.

I can't help but laugh at the exchange. It's obvious that these three men are great friends and Hope gives them as much crap as they give her and each other. Being an only child, I never had someone to banter with and I'm starting to think I missed out. My parents are wonderful people, but they are definitely quieter and more reserved than Hope. They still read the newspaper every morning, yes, the actual newspaper, not an online version. Every night they watch the news, a few game shows and go to bed by nine. I have a feeling Hope is the complete opposite.

"They are a mess," Isaac shakes his head at his teammates, "but I wouldn't know what to do without them."

"I take it you aren't a big partier."

"Sometimes in the off-season, but rarely during training and never once the season starts. The bar scene isn't for me.'

"I get that. I enjoy a drink or two, but I prefer to do it in the comfort of my home and with friends and family, not a bunch of drunks I've never met in a seedy bar."

"Agreed! I think we're going to be friends, Evan. I like the way you think."

The door is open. All I have to do is walk through it. Invite him over for a drink. He already wants to be friends and we think alike. Just do it.

Before I have a chance to talk myself out of it, I blurt out, "Would you like to come over for a drink tonight?"

Isaac stares at me, mouth open, a mix of confusion and shock on his face. *Stupid.* I should have kept my mouth shut.

I glance to the other side of the room, but Carter and Tyson are too busy razzing each other to have heard me. A glance in the other direction shows delight written all over Hope's face. She definitely heard me, and now I'm more than a little embarrassed. Shit. I have to learn to keep my mouth shut.

I'm about to take the invitation back when Isaac clears his throat. "Um, yeah, that would be great," he says almost in a whisper with a few glances to the other side of the room. I get the feeling he doesn't want anyone to know he just agreed to drinks at my place.

Hope looks away and busies herself cleaning her desk, but I see the smile on her face. At least someone is happy about my very uncomfortable current situation.

We spend the next few hours putting furniture together, unpacking boxes and setting up my office. While Tyson and Carter are in the other room talking to Hope, Isaac, and I exchange numbers and I give him my address. He seems a lot more interested and excited when it's just the two of us. Maybe I misread the signs and he isn't gay, or maybe he isn't out. Either way, I'm happy he's coming over tonight and looking forward to becoming friends. I'm definitely interested in more, but I can live with friends. I need one. Miami has been awfully lonely this past month.

EIGHT
ISAAC

Excitement courses through me as I pull into a parking spot outside of Evan's apartment. I still can't believe he asked me to come over tonight. I haven't been able to get him out of my head since he literally ran into me a few weeks ago. At first, I wasn't even sure he worked at the stadium. After a doing some digging online, I discovered he's the new Food and Beverage Coordinator, so when Carter asked me to help set up his office, I jumped at the opportunity. I was disappointed when we arrived this morning to discover Hope was surprising him and he likely wouldn't be coming by the office. Much to my surprise and enjoyment, he arrived less than twenty minutes after us. I was even more shocked when he asked me over but didn't ask anyone else.

After a quick look in the rearview mirror to check my hair, I make my way to his apartment on the third floor and knock. Seconds later the door swings open and Evan is standing there freshly showered, smelling like the beach, in a light-green button-down shirt with the first four buttons undone, showing off his gorgeous chest, and a pair of khaki cargo shorts. He's definitely spent some time outside since I ran into him a few weeks ago and the tan looks good on him. Damn, he looks as delicious as he smells.

Evan rakes his dark eyes, full of want and need, over my body before they meet mine.

"Come in," he squeaks out. Then quickly clears his throat as he steps back so I can enter. "Have a seat," he offers, motioning to the couch. "What can I get you to drink? I have a bottle of red wine one of my neighbors brought me, bourbon, water, and orange juice. Sorry, not many choices."

"What are you having?"

"Bourbon, neat."

"I'll have a bourbon on the rocks. I don't know how you drink it hot. I need the ice."

"It's room temperature, not hot," Evan tells me with a smile. "I'm something of a self-proclaimed bourbon connoisseur and cannot bring myself to ruin a good bourbon with ice, water or any kind of mixer, but I don't fault those who prefer it that way," he adds.

He pours our drinks and joins me on the couch.

"Okay, Mr. Bourbon Connoisseur, tell me what I'm drinking."

"This is a fifteen-year-old small batch bourbon from the Olde Derby Distillery outside of Louisville, Kentucky. It's one of my favorites. Very smooth with notes of caramel, vanilla, and a hint of spice."

"Damn, that's good," I express. He's right. This is one of the smoothest bourbons I've ever had. "I tend to stick to beer because it's easy and most of the time liquor just tastes nasty. Clearly, I've been drinking crap. This stuff is amazing," I admit.

"It is really good." Evan smiles, pleased with my reaction. "I'm happy to teach you about good bourbons. There is no reason to drink crappy liquor. What's the point? Well, unless your sole purpose is to get drunk then I guess drinking the cheap stuff is smart. Something like this is going to be upwards of forty or fifty bucks a shot in a bar. Another reason to enjoy it at home."

"Fair point. I'm not big on getting drunk. I like to remember my nights and prefer not waking up with a hangover."

"Me, too. Most nights if I pour a drink, I spend hours sipping on it."

"That's more my speed," I tell Evan, holding my glass up to clink with his.

Comfortable silence stretches between us as we enjoy sipping our bourbon. It's been a long time since I felt this relaxed around someone who caught my interest. Most of the time, I either get bored almost immediately or I'm an awkward bundle of nerves that can't shut up. With Evan, it feels different. I'm completely relaxed and don't feel the need to fill the silence by saying something stupid.

"How about some music or maybe a movie?" Evan asks.

"Sure. Either is fine with me."

Evan walks to the shelf next to the television and presses a button on a small black speaker then he connects his phone and quiet jazz music starts playing in the background. I'm glad he chose music. That way we can talk. I hate watching movies on a first date. Shit. As soon as the thought hits, I start backtracking in my head. This isn't a date. Sure, he asked me over for a drink, but we just met. I'm getting ahead of myself.

"Is this music okay? I can play something else."

"This is great."

I can listen to most any kind of music, but my personal

favorite is boy bands. They're kind of my guilty pleasure–anything from the Beatles to New Kids on the Block to One Direction. I love that shit. Of course, that's not something I'm sharing with someone I've only known a few hours. Hell, I might never tell him. It's not like anyone else knows except my younger brother and that's only because he came home early one night when we still shared a room and caught me dancing while belting out an NSYNC song. He never told anyone my secret, but he still makes fun of me.

"Do you like jazz?"

"I listen to pretty much anything. Mostly Pop, but I'm not against any music. What about you? Do you stick with jazz?"

"Mostly, yes. It has a calming effect on me. I'm not opposed to other music when someone else is choosing, but when I'm home alone, jazz is always my go-to."

"What do you like to do in your free time? Besides drinking damn good bourbon and listening to jazz?"

"The past few weeks, I've mostly been sleeping in my free time," he jokes. At first, I laugh, but when he doesn't laugh with me, my smile fades and I get serious. "When I have the time, I like to go for walks. I've driven out to the beach a few times since I've been here, but it's a little crowded for my taste."

"Yeah, the more popular beaches can get really crowded, but there are some quieter ones that aren't well known."

"I'll have to find one of those."

"I can show you sometime if you want."

"Yeah, that would be nice. Thanks."

"You said, you've been sleeping a lot. Is the job not going well?" I ask.

"The job is great, but it's new and I have a lot to learn. Before I moved here, I worked at the stadium in New Jersey as one of the food and beverage managers. The job was similar, but this is heading up all of the restaurants and bars instead of one or two. By the time I get home all I want to do is eat and go to bed."

"You're from New Jersey?" I ask. I probably should have recognized the accent.

"Yep. Born and raised in Rutherford."

"No shit. Me, too. Well, not Rutherford. I was born and raised in Edison."

"No kidding! That's cool."

"Do you ever get used to the heat?" Evan asks. "I miss the cold temperatures and I know once winter gets here, I'm going to wish for snow."

"The heat definitely gets old, and it never thinks about getting cold here. I miss my family but not the snow. I'd rather suffer through the heat than shovel another driveway."

"Not me. I absolutely love the snow and everything about it. Since I was old enough to hold a shovel, I've been shoveling our driveway, neighbors' driveways, and the sidewalk." Evan looks lost in amazing memories for a minute before shaking his head and continuing. "I'm going to miss it come November."

"I've never met someone who gets nostalgic over shoveling snow." I laugh and shake my head.

I like Evan. He's interesting and damn sexy. It has taken every ounce of willpower to keep my hands to myself all day and sitting on the couch next to him listening to him reminisce about our home state has me wanting to reach for him. My heart rate picks up a few notches, my hands begin to sweat, heat rushes through my body. What the hell is he doing to me? I've never felt this way about anyone, especially after only knowing him a few hours. I clear my throat and stand up.

"Bathroom?" I ask.

"Down the hall, first door on the left."

"Thanks," I croak.

I have to put some distance between us before I do something embarrassing like kiss him. I'm sure he's gay, but what if he isn't? What if he's being nice and trying to make friends in this new city? I guess if that was the case, he would have asked Tyson and Carter to join us, but he only asked me. I flush the toilet even though I didn't actually use it then I splash some cold water on my face and look in the mirror.

"Calm down," I whisper to my reflection. "You can do this. Either go out there and be his friend or make a move. What do you have to lose?" My personal pep talk does little to calm me as my anxiety ratchets up a few more notches. If I make a move, it could ruin the start of a friendship and I like hanging out with Evan. On the other hand, if I don't make a move, I'm going to keep torturing myself with what ifs. "You've got this. He's putting off interested vibes. Go for it." Anything is better than pretending to hit on girls at the club with Tyson and Carter, even if I'm wrong about the vibe I'm getting from him.

After drying my hands and face, I walk back to the other room. The apartment is small–one bedroom, one bathroom with a kitchen, eating nook, and living room all open to one another. There's a small balcony off the kitchen. I like Evan's place. It suits him. The couch is empty when I come out of the bathroom and with a quick glance to the right, I find him in the kitchen.

"Are you hungry? I'm going to make some pasta and a salad," he offers.

"Don't go to any trouble." I'm starving, but I don't want to put Evan out.

"It's no trouble. The pasta is one of those frozen dishes

with everything already in the bag. Basically, you put it in a pot, and it takes care of itself. The salad comes from a bag, too. Nothing to it."

"Sounds good to me. How can I help?"

NINE
EVAN

My heart melts when Isaac offers to help with dinner. I haven't dated much and the guys I usually date tend to be jerks. Apparently, in New Jersey, I had a type. It's time to change that. This is the first time I've had someone offer to help me cook. The last guy I dated expected me to wait on him. He owned a huge cyber security company and made more money in a year than I've made my whole life. To him, my job was menial. He always had something negative to say about how much I made. The best part about the move to Miami was he broke things off, but not before telling me I was making a huge mistake and I'd come crawling back to Jersey and him when I failed here. No matter what happens in Miami, I will never go back to him.

"Evan?" Isaac's voice cuts through my thoughts. "Where did you go?" Concern laces his words as he places a gentle hand on my back. Heat shoots through my body at his touch.

"Um, sorry, I'm here."

"Are you okay?" he asks, turning me to face him.

"Yeah." I wave him off and turn back to the freezer, but Isaac isn't having any of that. He turns me back to face him.

"Evan, what's wrong?"

I sign heavily, knowing I need to tell him something, but not sure if I want to lay myself open and bring up bad shit from my past.

I decide to be honest. "Sorry. When you offered to help, my mind immediately went to a bad place."

"Wanting to help is bad?"

"Not at all. Before I moved to Miami, I was in a bad relationship with someone who expected me to wait on him and take care of the cooking and cleaning up. He also made fun of me for not making as much money as him and called my job stupid and a waste of time. I guess having you offer to help was a little surprising." I look away as my face heats with embarrassment.

"That guy's an asshole," Isaac snaps. He turns me to face him and places a hand on each arm, looking me in the eyes. "No one should ever make you feel bad about who you are or what you do for a living. You offered to feed me dinner and I appreciate it. The least I can do is help. My parents raised me to be a gentleman and I don't expect anyone to wait on me." He smiles brightly. "Now, put me to work."

"Thank you." I tell him then hand him the bag salad. "There's a big blue bowl in the cabinet all the way to the left and a bag of croutons in the cupboard. Can you make the salad?"

"Of course. Do you have some dressing?"

"In the door of the refrigerator. I think I have a bottle of Caesar. If not, just use the open bottle of Italian."

While Isaac gets busy on the salad, I take out a large skillet, put two tablespoons of olive oil in the bottom and let it heat a little before pouring in the bag of pasta, vegetables, and chicken. As much as I enjoy cooking from scratch, these already prepared frozen meals have come in handy the past few weeks. Most nights, I would have skipped dinner if it wasn't for these.

Less than an hour later, we are sitting at the table with empty plates and full bellies. As I stand to clear the plates, Isaac stops me, "Sit. I'll take care of cleaning up."

"I can—"

"Evan," he cuts me off. "I want to clean up. You deserve a break."

"Thank you."

It's hard for me to let someone else take care of me. My parents are the only people who have ever done anything for me and for the last few years, I've made a point to do most of the cooking and cleaning. They were gracious enough to let me live in their home for five years after college before moving here. I tried to pay rent, but they refused to take my money, so I slowly started buying groceries, cooking, and cleaning. There was no way I was living there without doing something to help.

"Would you like another drink?" I offer.

"No. I have to drive soon."

"You can stay on the couch." The words are out of my mouth before I know I'm going to say them. What the hell? I can't believe I offered for him to spend the night. I barely know the guy. He's going to think I'm some kind of freak.

Isaac pauses for a few seconds as if letting the words sink in then he says, "If you don't mind having me crash here then I'd love another drink."

I nod to him then walk to the living room to retrieve our empty glasses. I can feel him watching my every move, so I refrain from smiling like an idiot or doing a happy dance in full view of the kitchen. It takes every single ounce of self-control to remain calm while I pour us each a double and bring his to him.

By the time I return to the kitchen, Isaac is loading the last few dishes in the dishwasher. I grab a pod from the container under the sink and hand it to him, then I spray and wipe down the counter, stove, and table. Once the cleaner is put away, we take our drinks and return to the couch. As soon as we sit down, Isaac takes my hand and lightning shoots through me. His touch sets every nerve on fire. I lace my finger through his and relax against the back of the couch, a smile tugging at my lips. I suspected Isaac was gay, but honestly thought he was just being friendly by accepting my invitation.

We stay like that for several minutes, holding hands and sipping our bourbon. I want to say something as the silence becomes uncomfortable, but I'm at a complete loss. Silence has never been easy for me. I feel like I need to fill it with words, music, the TV, anything. That's why I suggested music earlier. Isaac seems perfectly content with the silence, but I feel like I'm going to lose my mind.

Isaac must sense my discomfort because he slowly starts rubbing his thumb over my hand. My nerves immediately begin to calm. He takes my bourbon and sets both of our glasses on the coffee table. When he leans back, he's closer to me. Slowly, he leans toward me, invading my space. My breath hitches.

"Can I kiss you?"

I nod once before his lips are on mine. The kiss is gentle at first, then I open my mouth slightly and he pushes his tongue inside sending shock waves through me. Instinctively, I wrap my hands around him and rub them up and down his back, feeling every muscle through his shirt. Isaac follows suit wrapping one arm around me, pulling me closer while weaving the other hand into my hair.

Several breathless seconds later he pulls back and rests his forehead against mine.

"That was amazing," he says. "I haven't been able to get you out of my head since the first time we met."

"In the tunnel?" I ask. If that's what he's referring to, then he's been thinking about me as long as I've been thinking about him. That thought has me beaming.

"Yes." Isaac looks away as embarrassment heats his face.

Reaching up, I gently turn his face back to me and look him directly in the eye. "I've been thinking about you since that day, too," I admit.

"Really?" he questions and this confident man, who is one of the biggest names in the NFL, looks like a terrified little kid.

"Yes, really. The first time I saw you, I wanted to find a way to meet you again. When I showed up this morning, I was surprised to find you in my office."

"When Carter asked me to help, I jumped at the chance. I was disappointed when we first got there, and Hope told us it was going to be a surprise. I'm glad you decided to come into the office today."

Leaning in, I kiss Isaac this time. Not quite as passionately as he kissed me, but enough to show him how I feel.

"Me, too," I tell him after breaking the kiss.

We spend the next few hours, drinking bourbon and getting to know each other while holding hands and kissing. It's a damn good Saturday night. The best one I've had in a long time.

TEN
ISAAC

 On my last Sunday before the season starts, I open my eyes and smile. Not any smile, a big, goofy grin spreads across my face as I remember where I am and what happened last night. Waking up on Evan's couch is the best way to start the day. We talked and kissed until after two in the morning, but I feel great as I stretch and roll out my sore muscles then head for the bathroom. The couch is definitely too small for me, but I wasn't about to take him up on the offer to sleep in the bed while he took the couch, and it's too early in our relationship for me to share his bed. Relationship? Why the hell did I think that? We don't even know each other. Sure, we made out most of the night and hands wandered a little the more bourbon we drank, but I stopped myself before it went too far. I'm not one to jump in bed with someone I don't know. That's not entirely true. I have no problem with meaningless sex, but I like Evan and don't want to jeopardize what might happen between us by jumping into the sex part right out the gate.

A few minutes later when I emerge from the bathroom, Evan is in the kitchen with a fresh pot of coffee waiting.

"Good morning," he says with a smile that matches mine.

"Mornin'," I return, leaning in for a quick kiss. "Thank you for making coffee."

Evan pours each of us a mug and points to the cream and sugar he set out on the counter. After adding a little cream, I drop into one of the kitchen chairs.

"Any big plans today?" I ask.

"No. I'm going to force myself to relax. There is plenty of work to do and I probably should go into the office, but I'm trying to make myself take at least one day a week off."

"Good. You can't work constantly. You need a break."

"Do you have practice?"

"Not today. I have a workout session in an hour. After that, I'm free for the rest of the day. Do you want to do something together? I'd love to show you around Miami."

"Like a date?" He looks at me skeptically.

I think about that for a few seconds, letting the word *date* settle. This is what I want. I hope I'm not moving too fast. "Yes," I finally say. "I want to take you on a date."

"I would love that."

"Great! I'll be back around eleven to pick you up. We can grab a quick bite at one of the food trucks near the beach."

"Sounds good to me."

"See you in a few hours," I say after kissing Evan on the cheek and placing my empty mug in the sink.

Memories of last night flood my mind on the drive home. The first thought that hits me is his story about the way his ex treated him. Anger immediately courses through me. How can anyone treat sweet Evan that way? I wish I could have protected him from experiencing such a bad relationship. I take a calming breath. That man is in Evan's past and there's nothing I can do about it except make damn sure I never do those things to him. If I ever meet his ex, I will tell him just what I think of him.

Moving away from thoughts that are pissing me off, I switch to our upcoming date and a smile plays at my lips. Now that I've invited Evan out for the afternoon, I need something besides yesterday's clothes. I always keep extra workout clothes in the car, but I'm down to my last set and they're going to smell disgusting by the time my workout is over.

Fortunately, my neighborhood is between Evan's apartment and the gym, so I make a quick stop and rush back out the door. Since I'll be with Evan later and won't have time to call my parents, I decide to make the call now. Sunday is always our day to talk no matter how busy the week gets.

"Son, good to hear from you," Dad answers the landline they insist on keeping. "Putting you on speaker phone," he tells me as if I don't know they do this for every call.

"Hi, baby," Mom adds. "Why are you calling so early?"

"I'm on my way to the gym and have plans this afternoon, so I thought I'd call now."

"What kind of plans?" If I could see her face, I'd likely see a smile and wink.

"Mom," I reprimand. "It's just plans. Don't get too excited."

"Okay, okay." Mom chuckles. How does she always know? I said nothing to give her the impression my plans are of any significance. "Does he have a name?" she prods.

"Gloria, leave that boy alone," Dad scolds.

"It's okay, Dad. She isn't going to let it go until I give up the information."

"See, Jose, I know my boys. Now, let's have it, mijo."

"His name is Evan and we met yesterday. He works at the stadium. Last night, we had dinner and after my workout I'm showing him around Miami. That's it. He's a friend." I say pointedly, but it doesn't matter. Mom jumps on the little info I provide.

"Is he cute? Is this a date?"

"He's gorgeous and yes, today is a date. I don't know where this is going, but I like him," I admit.

Mom is the one person I can talk to about anything. She and Dad are both good listeners and give great advice. I don't have a problem talking to my dad about dating, but I'm more comfortable with Mom when the subject comes up.

"Oh, mijo, I'm so happy for you. I can't wait to hear all about your date."

"Don't get ahead of yourself. We just met."

"Too late," Dad says with a laugh. "She'll be planning your wedding by tonight."

"That's not true!" Mom responds. "I'll wait until after the second date."

"How's New Jersey? What game are you coming to this season?" I ask, desperate to change the subject.

"Things are great here. We got Aiden moved back to school. Katie started kindergarten and loves it," Mom gushes.

There's a quick pause and I hear some papers shuffling in the background. "Here it is," Dad mumbles. "Okay, we're coming to the Dolphins/Jets game the last week in October. We fly in on Thursday afternoon and fly home Tuesday morning. The extra days will give us some time to spend with you. Aiden doesn't have any classes on Friday this semester, so he will be with us from Friday to Monday. Owen and the girls are coming, too," Dad explains.

"Oh, wow! It will be like a mini family reunion! I wasn't sure Owen and Aiden would make it down this year."

"They aren't going to miss a chance to see you," Mom says.

"I'm at the gym. I need to go. Send me your arrival times and I'll either pick you up or send a car, depending on practice."

"I'll send it this afternoon," Dad agrees. "Bye, mijo. I love you."

"Love you, Dad. Bye, Mom. I love you."

"I love you, baby."

I end the call, grab my gym bag and head inside. Most of the team is already here. I'm not late, but I'm pushing it. I rush into the locker room and change quickly before doing some stretches.

Memories of last night flood my mind as I warm-up on the treadmill. I enjoyed being with Evan. We think a lot alike and have a few things in common. The best part was the kissing. It's been a long time since I kissed someone like that. The last few years have been about sex and taking care of my needs not relationships. There's little talking or kissing involved. I prefer talking and kissing. It's more intimate.

After thirty minutes on the treadmill, I hit the weight machines. Tyson has been eyeing me for the past several minutes with an odd look on his face. What is that all about? When I drop the dumbbell, barely missing my left foot, he jogs over to me.

"Are you okay?" he whispers.

"Yeah. Why?"

"Because you almost tripped on the treadmill twice and

that dumbbell you dropped missed your foot by centimeters. You can't afford a broken foot. You seem off."

"I'm not off," I snap. Then take a calming breath. It's not his fault I keep my sexuality a secret and now I've got to figure out how to approach whatever is happening between Evan and me. "Sorry. I'm tired. That's all."

He eyes me warily for several seconds before nodding and returning to his weight bench. He doesn't believe me, but he also knows if I need to talk, I'll come to him. I appreciate him giving me some space.

The rest of the workout goes a little smoother with no more near mishaps. After a quick shower, I'm heading back to Evan's and getting more and more excited with each passing mile.

ELEVEN
EVAN

 A glance at the clock on the microwave tells me I'm running out of time. Isaac will be here in a few minutes, and I'm not dressed. After eating a small breakfast, I showered and brushed my teeth, but I'm still sitting here in a pair of gym shorts, trying to decide what to wear. I finally gave up on the pile of clothes on my bed and came to the kitchen for a glass of water.

I've never had trouble figuring out what to wear on a date. I've also never been this nervous. I consider texting Isaac and requesting a rain check, but I don't want to do that to him. Even though I'm nervous, I'm excited about spending the day with him. He's a big deal in Miami and he's not out, which means we won't be holding hands or kissing. We both know it's a date and that's what's most important, but we will have to behave like two friends. I'm overthinking the whole situation. It's not as if I'm a big proponent of PDA. Even though my sexuality isn't a secret, I like my privacy and respect Isaac's. The topic of dating hasn't come up with anyone I've met here other than Isaac, so my new colleagues don't actually know I'm gay. *Today will be fine,* I assure myself. Two friends enjoying an afternoon together. I can do this.

After my silent pep talk, I walk back to the bedroom and pull on a pair of khaki shorts and a navy polo shirt. I want to look nice, but the heat is stifling. After I slip my feet into a pair of loafers, I put away all the clothes I tossed everywhere when trying to make a decision earlier. As I'm hanging up the last few shirts, the doorbell rings. I do one last look in the mirror to ensure I look okay before going to let Isaac in.

"Hey," I greet as soon as I swing the door open.

He rakes his eyes over my body sending a shiver down my spine. Today may be harder than I thought. Isaac pushes me against the wall, and I hear the door close behind him as he crashes his mouth onto mine. The kiss is rough and needy, and I love everything about it. Isaac's hands find their way to my hair as I wrap mine around him, pulling him flush against me, so I can feel every muscle against my chest. He pulls on my hair, and I moan into him. Damn he feels and tastes good. Isaac pushes against me, showing me just how turned on he is, causing me to moan again. Maybe we should skip this date and stay here after all. Before I can finish the thought, Isaac pulls back.

"All I thought about for the past three hours was getting back here so I could kiss you."

"It was worth the wait."

"Are you ready to go? I'm getting hungry."

"Ready." I grab my keys from the hook by the door and follow Isaac out to his car.

Before pulling out of my apartment complex, Isaac connects his phone to his car and pulls up his favorite playlist. I know because the playlist title *Favorite Playlist* shows on the dashboard screen. A song I don't recognize plays through the speakers. The title and artist show on the screen. Last night after a few drinks, Isaac admitted that he likes boy bands, so I'm not surprised it's a One Direction song. I definitely have to do some research into his music taste if we're going to spend time together. Before last night, I couldn't name a single boy band. Isaac pulls onto the highway, and we wind our way east toward the beach.

A few minutes into the ride, I find myself tapping my foot to his music. Surprisingly, I actually like the stuff he's playing. I've never been adventurous with music, but I might have to start trying some new genres.

Isaac reaches over and takes my hand, holding it as we continue driving. He glances my way several times. His features are tight. His body is stiff. He's definitely wound up about something.

"Are you okay?" I finally ask when he doesn't say anything.

"Uh-huh," he mumbles.

"Isaac, talk to me. Something is bothering you."

"I'm sorry, Evan. I want to spend time with you and I'm looking forward to this date, but..." he trails off, not finishing his thought. I wait several seconds before I finish for him.

"You're not out." He nods as a guilty look flashes across his face. "You told me last night. It's okay not to be out. Your personal life is no one's business and if you don't want the media to run with that kind of story, you should keep it private."

"That means we can't do this," he shakes our joined hands, "Once we're out of the car."

"I understand."

"We can't kiss," he continues.

"I know."

"We have to act like we're nothing more than two friends

hanging out. In the likely event that I get recognized, you might have to step aside while I take photos. There may even be some flirting involved with women we pass."

"Isaac," I say firmly, getting him to stop talking, "I understand all of this, and I knew these things, well, not the flirting with women part, but everything else. I knew all of that when I said yes to the date. I understand why you aren't out and would never do anything to make it appear like we're more than friends in public. It's not my place to decide if and when you come out. Only you can make that decision, and I will support you no matter what you decide."

Isaac breathes a huge sigh of relief as his features soften and his muscles relax. "Thank you. I rarely date for that reason. There are a few private clubs where discretion and privacy are required, but it's hard to find someone who wants a relationship at one of those clubs. Most of the men are looking for a hookup, nothing more. The last guy I dated lost his shit on me when I told him I wanted to keep things private, and then he threatened to expose me. That was three years ago. I haven't been on a date since. I hit one of the clubs to take care of my needs then go home alone."

"That's terrible. What a jerk for doing that to you. I see why you are worried about today and how things will go with us. No matter what happens between us, you never have to worry about me revealing your secret. Even if things don't work out."

"I appreciate you saying that, Evan. From the talks we had last night, I believed you felt that way which is why I was eager to take you out. As the morning went on and my excitement grew, so did my anxiety. Then the voices screaming at me to take you home and not trust you, got a little too loud. You're not like most guys I meet. I never know if people like me or my status."

"I'd like you even if you weren't some football god. That's just an added bonus," I tease, causing him to laugh.

"Football god," he repeats, reverence in his voice. "I like it."

"I'm not calling you 'god,'" I deadpan, causing him to laugh even harder.

He sobers and firmly says, "Don't be so sure about that."

Aaaand now I'm hard. The smirk on Isaac's face tells me he knows exactly what he did.

"Payback's a bitch," I mumble with a satisfied smirk as Isaac busts out laughing. Challenge accepted.

TWELVE
ISAAC

The area I want to show Evan is more crowded than usual. We drive around for almost fifteen minutes before getting lucky and finding a parking spot in the lot closest to where the food trucks usually park. Thankfully, I did a second pass through the lot as someone was pulling out. I pay at the kiosk then fall in step next to Evan. The September sun beats down on us and I'm grateful I opted for shorts and a T-shirt instead of jeans. It never gets cold in Miami, but at least in the winter months, the humidity isn't quite as bad.

We walk two blocks north and turn right toward the beaches. As soon as we turn, we are met with a packed street. Several city blocks are barricaded, and vendors are set up along the street. I forgot it was Labor Day weekend and they were having the street festival today. No wonder I had trouble finding a parking space.

"What's all this?" Evan asks with a look of amazement.

"Street festival. They have it most holiday weekends," I

explain. "Do you want to look at some of the booths?" I ask him.

"Absolutely!" Evan takes off toward the one closest to us, weaving through a few people to get a closer look. It takes me a minute to catch up to him because I get stopped twice for photos. When I reach Evan, he is talking to the vendor about some old WWII photograph.

"My dad was a journalist during the war. These are prints of some of the photos he took," the man explains.

"They're fantastic. I'll take these two," Evan says, handing the prints to the gentleman. "My dad will love them. He's a history buff, especially anything to do with war and he loves planes."

"Would you like them framed?"

"No, thank you."

The man wraps the photos in tissue paper even though they are already in sealed plastic sleeves, then carefully places them in a bag.

"That'll be thirty dollars. I take cash or cards."

Evan hands over his credit card and the man completes the transaction. "Thank you. Have a nice day."

"You, too." Evan smiles and waves as we start toward the next booth.

"Sorry about that. I had to take a few pictures and sign some autographs."

"It's no problem. Part of being a big football god is catering to the fans," he teases me with a flippant wave. All I can do is smile and shake my head. I like that he gives me shit in a fun, teasing way.

"Was your dad in the military?" I ask, nodding to the bag.

"No, but he loves to watch war documentaries. I think sometimes he regrets not joining, but he married my mom right after high school and went to work in a factory."

"Wow, they got married young."

"Yeah, eighteen, but they didn't have me for almost ten years. I'm an only child and I've often wondered why they waited so long."

"You never asked?"

"No. I'm not sure I want to know. If they wanted kids, but struggled, I don't want to bring up bad memories. If they never wanted children and I was an accident, I don't think I want to know."

"It's possible they always planned to have one child and waited until they were older so they could grow up together first. It might be a happy, positive story."

"You're right and I've thought that, too. I guess I figured if it was a story worth telling, they would have shared it with me."

We glance at the next few booths, but nothing catches our interest until we get to one selling vinyl. I have to take a look. Evan follows me and immediately finds the section labeled Jazz while I look for Pop. There are a few Beatles albums that I don't have so I choose one. By the time I meet Evan at the checkout table, we both have several albums in hand.

"Do you have a record player?" I ask. It's a stupid question. Why would he be buying records if he has no way to play them?

"Actually, no. These two are for my mom," he says, showing me a Dolly Parton album and a Christmas hits album with some of the most iconic female singers of all time.

"What about that one?"

"It's for me. I moved with a small collection of vinyl, but since the only player we had at the house belonged to my parents, it stayed in Jersey. Purchasing one has been on my to-do list since I moved, but it keeps getting pushed to the back burner."

"We definitely have to fix that soon."

We make our purchases and meander past a few more booths. No one else stops me, but I get a few waves and some 'Go Dolphins' as we weave through the crowd. We are close to the end of the vendors and a sea of food trucks rests in the next block.

"Are you hungry?" Evan asks, eyeing the trucks.

"Starving."

"Good. Let's eat."

After a short discussion we settle on a Mac's Seafood truck, serving fish tacos and lobster macaroni and cheese. We order one of each with a side of chips and guacamole and four bottles of water. He packs the food in a to-go bag and hands it to Evan while I pay. Evan offered to pay, but I refused. I asked him out, so today is my treat.

"Come on." I nod my head to the right and start toward the beach. "I know the perfect place to enjoy our lunch."

Leading the way, I take Evan to North Shore Beach about a half-mile down the street. It's a beautiful strip of white sand and tends to be off the tourist radar. Usually, it's pretty quiet and laid back. When we arrive, I stop at the rental booth and get us two chairs and an umbrella. We find a spot near the end of the strip where no one else is sitting right now. Most people are back on Miami Beach near the food trucks and vendors, so I don't expect it to get much busier here.

"This is beautiful," Evan gushes, taking a seat and divvying up the food. "I can't believe it isn't packed here."

"It never is. Most people stay near the beaches close to hotels and restaurants."

"It's the perfect place for a private lunch. Good call."

We fall into comfortable silence as we devour the tacos,

chips, and macaroni. Mac's Seafood is my favorite food truck in the area, so I was ecstatic to see it at the festival. After we eat, Evan kicks his shoes off and runs for the water.

"What are you waiting for?" he tosses over his shoulder.

I can't help but laugh at his antics as he runs into the small waves. He kicks his feet, splashing water and drenching the bottom half of his shorts. I'm not a huge fan of the ocean, too many things can go wrong. Pushing my reservations aside, I leave my shoes next to the chair and run to join Evan. As long as I don't go too far out, I'll be fine.

As soon as I'm next to him, he kicks one foot then the other at me, making my shorts as wet as his.

"Can you believe how warm the water is here?" he practically squeals with excitement.

"Yeah, I can," I chuckle.

"Oh, huh, I forgot you've lived here for six years."

"First time in warm tropical waters?"

"Yep. The water in Jersey never gets truly warm and it's probably been ten years since I've been to a beach."

Ten years. Wow. I'm not sure why that surprises me so much. I rarely visited a beach before I moved here, but now it seems so odd to hear someone say they never go to the beach. I come out here to relax at least once a week even though I don't go in the water.

When we are both thoroughly drenched, Evan runs back onto the sand and drops to his knees. At first, I think something is wrong, so I rush to his side. When I get there, he is packing sand into small squares.

"What are you doing?"

He looks at me like I've lost my mind, "Building a sand-castle," he says it as if the most normal thing in the world for a grown man to be kneeling in the sand building his own castle. I guess it isn't that uncommon. There are huge sand-castle building contests around the world.

Deciding that he's having way too much fun without me, I park myself next to him and start making my own squares. "Do you have a plan?"

"Not at all," Evan laughs. "Stack the squares to make walls?" He says it as a question, so I agree and start stacking.

By the time we have the third wall built, it's beginning to look a little like a building. Evan starts a new wall, coming off one of the three completed ones, but not closing the fourth wall. When he notices me staring at him with a raised brow, he shakes his head.

"We can't have a one room castle." It sounds as if he can't believe I didn't understand that piece of information, which I didn't.

"Alright. Since you're the master architect, how many rooms are we making?"

"Ten," he says with confidence. "On the first floor."

"Ten? First floor? You really are building a castle."

"Well, yeah, go big and all that." He waves his hand as if it makes perfect sense.

This guy is amazing. If someone would have told me a week ago, I'd be spending today building a sandcastle with the hottest guy I've met in a long time and enjoying every second while falling very hard and very fast, I would have laughed in their face and called them crazy.

THIRTEEN
EVAN

I'm starting to doze off when I feel the car stop and hear Isaac chuckle softly beside me. I open my eyes suddenly alert. Shit. We're back at my apartment already.

"Sorry," I mumble.

"It's fine. You had a big day. Building an entire castle takes its toll on one."

"Are you making fun of me?" I ask in mock horror, holding a hand to my chest.

"Not at all. You had a busy day."

"That castle was three stories!" I exclaim.

"I'm aware."

"It had a moat!"

"It did."

Isaac tries to keep a straight face but fails miserably, leaning forward and laughing a deep, loud belly laugh that goes straight to my dick. He gets out of the car and rushes around to my side, opening the door before I have a chance. I'm enjoying the whole gentleman thing he's been doing all

66

day. We didn't hold hands or act like more than friends, but all day he's done little things like open my door and buy me lunch to show he cares.

I gather my bags from the festival and climb out of the car. Starting for the elevator, I glance back to make sure Isaac is following me. I should have invited him in, but when I look behind me, he is hot on my heels. Good. Even though I'm tired, I'm not ready for the date to end.

We take the elevator to my floor. Usually I walk the three flights, but I'm too tired for that tonight. "Come in," I offer as I open the door. He steps past me and walks into the apartment.

I lock the door and head down the hallway. "Make yourself at home. I'll be right back."

After using the bathroom and washing my hands and face, I change into some clean clothes. We both rinsed off at the outdoor beach showers, but our clothes are still wet. I need a real shower, but that can wait a few more minutes. I grab some clothes for Isaac and a bottle of bourbon that I've been dying to try.

"Here's some clothes if you want to put on something dry."

"Thank you. I'm not sure how much longer I can handle these wet shorts and my only change of clothes is pretty nasty from my workout this morning."

"After you change, why don't you grab the dirty clothes from your car and we can wash them along with the wet ones," I suggest.

"Are you sure? I can wait until I get home."

"It's no problem. I have a few things I can throw in to make a full load."

"Sounds good to me." Isaac takes the clothes from me and retreats to the bathroom.

By the time he returns, I have two glasses of bourbon poured for us, the oven is preheating and I'm pulling pizzas out of the freezer. He pulls my back against his chest, kissing my cheek.

"What's all this?"

"This is a bourbon that I bought last year and have been saving to enjoy with someone special," I say, handing him a glass of the brown liquid. I point to the open freezer, adding, "And this is going to be dinner."

Isaac closes the freezer door, leaving me empty handed then wraps his arms around me. He turns me around and sets his glass on the counter next to mine. He takes my face in his hands and looks deep into my eyes as if he can see straight into my soul and read all my thoughts.

"Today was perfect. I had a great time and look forward to many, many dates with you." He kisses me gently at first then deeper. I lean into the kiss and open my mouth for him. I moan as he pushes his erection into mine and the kiss becomes frantic with need. Hands are everywhere. His mouth goes from my lips to my ear to my neck. My breathing is heavy, and I need him. I need him so fucking much right now.

He sucks on my neck as I rub my hand down his chest to his crotch, rubbing his erection through his shorts.

"Please," I beg.

"What do you want?"

"You. I want you." My words are breathless and needy.

"Are you sure?"

"Yes."

Isaac reaches behind me and turns the oven off before taking my hand and leading me toward the bedroom. This is happening. Seriously. This is happening right now and I'm freaking the hell out. It's been almost a year since I've been with a man. The guy I was dating before I moved hadn't been interested in sex for months. I'm sure he was cheating on me. I guess I wasn't enough for him. I can't admit that to Isaac. He'll think I'm a loser. I want him, but I'm not sure I'm ready for this.

What the hell am I going to do? If I reject him, he's going to be mad. He must see the conflict on my face when he turns me toward him.

"What's wrong?

"Nothing." I shake my head. My words aren't convincing. I can hear the skepticism loud and clear.

"Sit," he commands, taking a seat on the bed and patting the mattress. "Tell me what's wrong. This," he points at me, "is not the same Evan who was in the kitchen."

I hang my head. This is it. This is where I tell him the truth and run him off or do something I'm not ready for yet.

Isaac lifts my chin and looks me in the eyes. "You can tell me anything."

I opt for the easy way out instead of bringing up the fuckery that was my relationship with Mike. "I'm not very experienced and I'm not sure I'm ready for this step."

"We don't have to do anything you don't want to do."

"You're this famous football star who can get anyone he wants. I'm a workaholic, who lived with his parents until a few months ago."

"One, I haven't been with as many people as you might think. Two, I don't care how much experience you have or don't have. This is about us and what we want, not about our past. I'll never judge you for not knowing something or not having a certain experience. Do you think it bothers me that you're not a football player?"

"No. That doesn't make any sense. We have different jobs."

"Exactly. How many people we've slept with is no different. Do you care how many guys I've screwed?"

"No."

"Good. I don't care how many you've been with, either."

I hang my head again. Why am I so messed up? Why can't I enjoy the moment instead of getting in my own head and sabotaging something great?

"How about we eat some dinner and take the sex part of our relationship a little slower?"

"Relationship?" Is he implying that there is something more between us?

"I hope so. If you'll have me, I'd like us to be exclusive," he admits with a shy smile that surprises me coming from Isaac.

"Yes. I'd like that."

"Good. Then there is no reason to rush the sex part. It will happen when we're both ready. Let's go get some food."

Isaac stands, but I grab his hand before he can walk away. He turns to face me, "Thank you, Isaac."

I worry that the rest of the night will be uncomfortable, but Isaac seems perfectly happy doing our laundry and making dinner with me. It's all very domestic. We cook a couple of frozen pepperoni pizzas, adding spices, mushrooms, and peppers to them. It makes me smile when Isaac agrees with the toppings. I love almost anything on a pizza even anchovies and once in a while pineapple. Isaac gagged when I suggested anchovies and said pineapple should never go on a pizza. I strongly disagreed, but at least we settled on a few toppings we both enjoy.

The sex topic doesn't come up again and the entire evening is fun and relaxing. By the time we eat and clean up the kitchen, it's after eight. I'm not nearly as tired as I was when we first got home.

"Are you up for a movie?" I ask as I put the last dish away.

"Sure. Do you have something in mind?"

"Well, I was thinking we could take a quick shower then snuggle up in my bed and watch a comedy. That way, if we fall asleep, we'll be comfortable."

"Are you sure? I don't want to push you."

"I'm confident we can take a shower without having sex. And I'd like to have my boyfriend in my bed with me."

"I'd like that very much." Isaac smirks, taking my hand and practically pulling me down the hallway.

FOURTEEN
ISAAC

 Preseason is over and our first game is starting in a little over an hour. The locker room is buzzing with excitement, reporters and photographers have been in and out all morning, interviewing players and taking photos.

I'm suited up and ready to head to the field for warmups. Nerves ate away at me last night and all morning. That always happens before the first regular season game and again if we make the playoffs. It's been part of my routine since I was a kid, so I guess it's my body's way of preparing me for the game in some weird fashion.

Once I got to the stadium and into my uniform, I felt the anxiety start to melt away. Running out onto the field changes everything. As soon as my cleats hit the turf, I feel relaxed and confident. I glance up toward the employee box, knowing I can't see anything from here and knowing Evan is working and won't be watching me play today.

I can't get enough of that man. He's becoming an important part of my daily life and I can't imagine not being with him. I also can't understand how he embedded himself into my life so easily. It feels like we've known each other for years even though it's only been two weeks since our first date. We see each other almost every night and I'm already dreading the away game next week. It's going to be hard to be away from him for two nights. If we have a day game, we fly back after, but since next week is a night game, we'll leave Miami Saturday evening and return Monday morning. Then I have to wait until Evan gets off work to see him.

As I find my spot near the ten-yard line and begin to stretch, I shake away thoughts of Evan. It's time to focus on today's game instead of worrying about what will happen next week.

The Jaguars start warming up on the other end of the field as I finish my stretches and run from one end of the end zone to the other several times. This should be an easy win, but I'm trying not to let my confidence go to my head. Getting cocky before the game even starts is a recipe for disaster. I've seen great teams lose to the worst team in the league. Confidence is good, but cockiness can be detrimental.

When our warmup time is over, Tyson jogs beside me back to the locker room for a final word of encouragement from our head coach. He doesn't say anything to me, simply jogs beside me. Tyson is in his own head by now, going over plays and giving himself a private pep talk. This is his routine for every game. He'll joke around and have fun at practice, but on game day, he is quiet and stoic. He rarely speaks to anyone in the hour before the game starts. We respect his need for calm and quiet before the games and give him the space he needs.

On the contrary, I'm usually joking around with some of the other guys on the team, cutting up, giving interviews, and encouraging anyone who's struggling. Today is different. I'm wrapped up in thoughts of Evan and can't seem to focus on the conversations around me or the speech coach is finishing. I have no idea what he said in the last five minutes. Hope it wasn't anything important.

Running back onto the field this time is completely different. The stands are full now, and the cheers erupting around the stadium are deafening. Blocking out the noise, I walk onto the field with Tyson and Mark Sharkey. We're the captains today and will be representing the team for the coin toss.

We win the toss and choose to kick, giving the Jaguars the ball first. It's a smart plan that will allow us to have the ball first in the second half. I find a place on the sidelines to watch the beginning of the game. Carter walks up next to me. With Tyson at quarterback, Carter won't get much play time unless we have a huge lead or Tyson gets hurt. Carter's good, but not many quarterbacks in the league are as good as Tyson.

"You ready?" he asks.

"More than you know."

I only played in two preseason games for about a quarter of each game. Coach didn't want to chance the seasoned players getting hurt before game one, so we saw very little game time. It gave Carter the chance to play while Tyson sat on the bench and he proved his worth, helping us win three of the four preseason games. I'm impressed with him and feel confident in his ability if we lose Tyson for any reason.

Three minutes later our defense forces a punt and it's time for me to take the field. That was easy. Let's see if our offense can score in the next three minutes. I take my position on the O line. The ball is snapped and as Tyson steps back, I push a couple of Jaguars defensive lineman out of the way and run several yards down the field. Tyson sees me open and sails the ball through the air into my waiting arms. No one is near me as I take off running toward the end zone. Keeping my eye on the goalpost, I block out everything around me, passing the forty-yard line. Thirty. Twenty. Ten. Touchdown! Mark is the first teammate to reach me.

"Fuck, yeah!" he yells with a high five. Others congratulate me as I jog back to the sidelines.

Tyson meets me there, slaps my ass, and says, "That's the way to do it, boy. We've got a rhythm!"

He says it as if we haven't had a rhythm for the past six years. Tyson and I click and have one of the strongest quarterback/receiver relationships in the league. It's like we're one mind on the field. He can sense where I'm going to be and always finds me even when I'm not completely open. We can read each other well enough for him to know when he should throw it to me and when he needs to find someone else.

By the middle of the second quarter, we're up 17-0. The offense is on the field again, hoping to increase our lead to 24 before the half.

The Jaguars' defense has stepped up their game this quarter and after the snap, I find myself in a shit-ton of Jaguar traffic. Tyson is backing away from two of their players. He bounces left then right before being sacked. Shit.

We line up, second and eighteen. The ball is snapped, and I find myself in the same position as the last play. Tyson is faring better and finds an open receiver. Mason misses the catch to bring up third and eighteen. Not a good place to be. We need a first down. This time, I fake left then rush right and get around the mass of bodies trying to block me. Tyson throws the ball, and it lands in my hands. I'm tackled a few yards later, but it's enough for a first down. We still have a ways to go to get to the end zone, but we're in a much better position and we have four more downs.

Tyson gets sacked on the next two plays then Coach calls a

timeout. He pulls a very frustrated Tyson from the game and puts Carter in.

"Bring it home, Masters," Coach calls as we jog back onto the field.

"You've got this," I encourage as I pass Carter to take my position. The Jaguars are lined up evenly along the line, probably hoping to block as many of us as possible since we've faked them out a few times. It might not matter. Our guys are frustrated with the lack of progression with this latest drive. Carter catches the ball when it's snapped, takes three steps back, and gets sacked hard. He doesn't get up. Damn. Fourth and fifteen, five seconds in the half, and an injured quarterback. Not the way we wanted to end the second quarter. I jog over to Carter before the medical staff gets there. His eyes are open, but he looks a little dazed.

"You okay?" I ask as he pushes himself into a sitting position.

"I think so. A little dizzy."

That's not good. I step aside while the medical staff takes over and checks him out. He walks off the field on his own, but it's pretty obvious he has a concussion. We punt the ball and the Jaguars run it out to the thirty-yard line before the clock hits zero.

The second half was a little more difficult than we thought it would be. The Jags definitely came to win. They scored three times in the third quarter. By the middle of the fourth, we were tied at 27. A little luck in the last few minutes of the game put us up by a touchdown and we won the game. The other team didn't make it easy. By the time I shower, check on Carter, and make it to my car, I'm exhausted. It's almost nine and the only thing I want to do is crawl in bed. I drive to Evan's apartment and knock on the door, hoping he's already home. I'm not sure how long he has to stay after the game to make sure everything is done for the night.

There's no answer, so I walk back to my car to call him, but he's pulling into the lot when I get downstairs.

"Hey, I didn't think you were coming by tonight," he says, climbing out of the car, locking it behind him.

"I thought about going straight home, but I wanted to see you." I follow him up the three flights of stairs and into his apartment.

"I'm glad you're here." Evan pulls me close to him and kisses me quickly. "Congratulations on the win." He steps out of my arms and walks to the kitchen, taking two bottles of water from the refrigerator and handing one to me.

"Thanks."

"Are you hungry?" he asks.

"No. I stopped at a drive thru after the game and ate on the drive here."

"Well, I'm starving. I haven't eaten since breakfast." Evan pulls out bread, meat, cheese, and mayonnaise and starts making a sandwich. "How's Carter? I heard he got hit hard. I texted Hope, but she hasn't responded."

"He has a concussion. No loss of consciousness, so that's good. He'll be okay in a couple of weeks."

"I'm glad he's going to be okay. I can't imagine how scary that must be for his family and teammates to watch."

"Yeah, it's the one part of the job I hate. I don't like to see anyone get hurt, whether they're on my team or the other."

Evan finishes his sandwich and cleans up the kitchen. Then he takes my hand, "Will you stay with me tonight? I have to get up early for work, but you can stay and sleep in if you want."

"I was hoping you'd ask me to stay," I say with a wink, taking his hand. "I'll take you up on the offer to sleep in. I have a team meeting at ten and then I'll work out for a few hours, but I have no desire to get up at six with you."

Evan smiles as he pulls me into the bedroom then we get undressed. He snuggles up against me and I relax into him. *Home* is the last thought I have as I doze off for the night.

FIFTEEN
EVAN

 We're three games into the season. I worked the first game, making sure food and drink service ran smoothly. Last week, the team was in California, so I had the weekend off. It was nice to have a break, but I missed spending my free time with Isaac.

Working six days a week for the past month has been brutal. It's left me completely exhausted. The apartment is a mess and Isaac and I haven't had near enough time together. Between his practice and travel schedule and my hours, we might as well be acquaintances. Good thing we make the most of the time we have together. He's spent many nights at my house, but we're like an old married couple–dinner and an early bedtime. We Facetime every night we don't get to see each other.

I have an amazing staff, and all my new employees are trained, so it's time for me to back off a little. My plan for the next few weeks is to work from home on Monday and at the stadium Tuesday through Friday. Then come in early on

Sunday to help get things prepared for the game and enjoy watching the game from the employee box in case I'm needed. Unless he's traveling, Isaac has Monday off with the exception of a workout and a team meeting. Maybe this adjustment in my schedule will afford us some more time together.

I'm shutting down my computer, so I can head to the employee box when there's a knock on the office door. I dread answering it because it's likely an issue with one of the restaurants or bars, which means I'll be working instead of watching my man on the field. I hate that I missed his first game and had to watch the second one alone in my apartment.

As slowly as possible I drag my feet to the door. When I pull it open, Isaac is standing on the other side, half dressed for the game minus the shoulder pads and jersey. He pushes me into the office and kicks the door closed behind him. His lips are on mine before I have a chance to register what's happening. My head is swimming as I get lost in the feel of his tongue against mine.

Too soon, he breaks the kiss, "I only have a minute. I snuck off after my warmup, but I had to see you before the game. My ass will be in deep shit if anyone realizes I disappeared this close to kick off."

"I'm glad you stopped by," I respond breathlessly. "But go before you get in trouble."

He ignores me and continues talking. "I brought you something." He smiles, handing me a small, wrapped box.

I tear into the wrapping paper. When it comes to presents, I'm like a kid on Christmas. I love gifts–giving and receiving. When I pull the lid off the box, I find a Dolphins' jersey. I hold it up, revealing the name Flores and the number 63 on the back.

"I thought you might want to wear it to the game."

"I'm wearing it to every game from now on!"

I toss the packaging on the ground then pull off my Dolphins T-shirt and replace it with Isaac's jersey. I have several Dolphins shirts and I keep thinking about buying a jersey with Isaac's name and number, but by the time I leave the office at night, I'm too tired to go shopping.

"Thank you."

"You're welcome. It looks good on you," Isaac all but growls.

The white compression shirt he wears under his jersey hugs every taut stomach and chest muscle. Slowly, I rub my hands over each muscle, reveling in the feel of his hard chest. Damn, I love this man's body. Leaning in, I kiss his neck then ear. He lets out a moan that's a mix of pleasure and frustration and it spurs me on. I lick his ear as one hand curls in his short, brown hair and the other crawls down his chest, lower and lower until I reach his cock only to be met with hard plastic. Fuck. I forgot about the cup. I decide to go a different route and snake that hand around his waist, squeezing his tight ass while my lips find his. I push my tongue inside and deepen the kiss while my other hand drifts to his ass, pulling him close so he can feel my hardness against his leg. Then I start rubbing on him, slow at first then faster. I can't believe I'm rubbing myself off on his leg.

Isaac groans then grabs my hair pulling gently before pushing me back while taking his own step backwards. His breathing is heavy, and his entire face is flushed. He reaches down and adjusts himself the best he can in those exquisitely tight pants and a cup.

"We have to stop or I'm going to miss the game," he growls.

"Is there a problem?" I ask in my most innocent voice.

"You know exactly what you're doing to me."

I smirk at him, "Yeah, payback's a bitch." I shrug then turn away and take a few steps as if dismissing him.

Two steps later, Isaac grabs my arm and spins me toward him. "You've been waiting for a moment like this for over a month?" he questions, sounding as impressed as he is frustrated.

"Hmm, you remember."

"I remember everything you've said from the moment I met you."

When I don't respond with anything other than a smirk, Isaac growls again, running a hand through his hair. "This isn't over. Wait until I get you home tonight."

"Is that a promise or a threat?" I challenge.

"Both."

Before I have a chance to register Isaac's last word, he's out the door. I rush to the hallway to call a goodbye to him and wish him a good game, but he's gone. Damn, he's fast. Closing the door behind me, I walk to the bathroom and splash some water on my face. What I need is an ice-cold shower, but this will have to do. Once I calm the hell down, I clean up the wrapping paper and turn off the lights before locking the door behind me.

The game starts in fifteen minutes, so I make my way to the box, grabbing a plate of food from the buffet and a drink from the bar before finding a seat near the window with a clear view of the entire field. This is amazing. I can see everything from up here. Many of the seats in the stadium are shaded, but the hot Florida sun beats down on the field. Even in October, temperatures can rise into the nineties mid-day. The Dolphins' players are used to playing in this heat, but the Bills players have to be miserable. I guess it's no different than our guys playing in the dead of winter up north. In this heat, I'm eternally grateful for the air-conditioned box.

It makes me wonder if I will love the cold as much when I visit home this winter as I did growing up. How long does it take to acclimate to a different climate? Will I ever be truly warm in the north again? These questions along with a bunch of very intimate thoughts of what Isaac meant by his last statement run through my head as I enjoy my plate of food.

"Hi!" a bubbly voice interrupts my thoughts. "Is this seat taken?'

"Uh, no," I respond, motioning for her to sit down.

"I'm Amelia. I work in marketing."

"Nice to meet you. I'm Evan. I'm the Food and Beverage Coordinator."

"Do you work with Hope?"

"Yeah, she's my assistant."

"She's wonderful. Hope's like the stadium Mom."

"I can see that. She keeps me grounded for sure."

"I'm her daughter." She pauses and waves another girl over. "This is my sister, Bethany."

"Great to meet you. So, you're Hope's daughters. I've been hoping to meet you both. I met Carter on my first day but haven't met Derron yet."

"You'll see a lot of Carter. He's the baby and such a momma's boy. Derron is the oldest and keeps himself busy. Sometimes, I think he forgets his entire family lives here and would like to see him once in a while."

"Hush your mouth, Beth," Amelia scolds. "Don't tell our family secrets."

"That's not a secret. Derron is too busy finding his latest hookup to be bothered with any of us."

"Bethany!" Amelia turns several shades of red and I can't help but smile at their banter. I never had siblings, but this is always how I imagined it would be if I had a couple of brothers or sisters.

"Is Hope coming today?" I ask in an effort to ease the tension.

"Yeah, she always stops by the locker room to see the boys before coming up here," Amelia informs me.

"She'll be glad to see you. We've gotten several earfuls about how much you work and how you need to take some time to relax."

"She's not wrong. I've always thrown myself into my job, but it's been worse since moving here. There's so much to learn and do. I would have run back to New Jersey weeks ago if it wasn't for Hope. She's the hardest worker I've ever known. I'm thankful for her."

"Stop that nonsense," Hope's sweet voice reaches me before I know she's behind me. "You are brilliant at your job. A hundred times better than Sandy. You're personable and your employees love you. The same cannot be said for Sandy. She was kind of a witch."

"What? Really?" I ask in shock.

"What surprises you? That you're an amazing boss or Sandy was the worst?" Hope asks with a gleam of humor in her eyes.

I think about her question for a second. "Um, both, I guess."

"Well, trust me when I tell you that you are a wonderful boss, and your reviews are spectacular. Sandy's employee rating on her best day was a 2.5 out 5 stars. All of your reviews are 4s and 5s."

"What are you talking about? What reviews?"

Hope pales and stumbles over a few words before she's able to form a complete sentence. "Sandy didn't tell you? That figures. She thought the rating system was a bunch of bullshit, but I think that's because no one had anything positive to say about her."

"That doesn't actually explain anything," I tell Hope as a pit forms in my stomach. I'm not good with criticism and if there's a chance my employees are being mean to me, I might lose it.

"You have nothing to worry about," she comforts, patting my arm. "There is a tab in the employee portal where you can rate your boss and other employees. The reviews go straight to the general manager's office, but you can see your ratings and any review that an employee marked as public. I've read some of your reviews, and they are all positive. You have one of the highest ratings of any manager or coordinator in the stadium. People love you!"

My mind boggles at Hope's words. There is no way she is serious. I have to check out this portal thing when I get home. Before I have a chance to question Hope further, a voice comes over the loudspeaker asking us to stand for the National Anthem. We all stop talking and stand for the song. After we sing, cheers erupt around the stadium as the players run onto the field.

Miami has the ball first, so the offense and my hot boyfriend are on the field. The Bills kick off and Tate Grimes catches the ball near the end zone and runs it to the thirty yard-line before getting tackled by two Bills' players.

Miami lines up and the ball is snapped. Tyson falls back a few steps, looking for someone open. Isaac is about fifteen yards away, wide open. Tyson makes eye contact and launches the ball into the air. Isaac easily makes the catch without even slowing down. He catches the ball mid-run and keeps going–forty, fifty, forty, thirty, twenty. He's tackled just inside the twenty-yard line. Damn, that was a good run.

Two plays later, the Dolphins are first and goal on the five-yard line. Less than three minutes into the game and it's already the most exciting game I've ever watched. That probably has a little something to do with watching Isaac play.

"Tyson Sanders falls back," the announcer calls, "He's looking for a receiver. Bills have great coverage. Pressure is on Sanders as he looks desperately for an open receiver. Griffin gets the sack, setting Miami up for second and goal!" he bellows across the stadium.

Next play, Tyson steps back. Isaac is open in the end zone. He overshoots and the ball lands out of bounds. Frustration pours off him. Isaac runs over to Tyson and leans into him, helmet to helmet, saying something no one can decipher. Isaac claps Tyson on the shoulder and runs to his position on the line. The ball is snapped, Tyson steps back, Isaac fakes right then runs left leaving two Bills players barely passing each other without a collision. By the time the Bills realize what's happened, Isaac is in the end zone with the ball secure in his grasp.

"Touchdown Dolphins!" the announcer yells as the crowd goes completely wild.

My man just scored the first touchdown of the game, much like the first game of the season. I beam with pride that I hope comes across as joy for the team and not pride for my sexy boyfriend. We're still keeping our relationship quiet, and I don't want anyone to question my enthusiasm, especially while I'm wearing a Flores jersey.

The rest of the half is just as exciting. The Bills answer our touchdown with one of their own and the two teams go back and forth for the first half, leaving it tied at 21 before heading to the locker room at half time.

SIXTEEN
ISAAC

 The past two weeks have been busy for both Evan and me with the start of the season. We beat the Bills yesterday by a field goal in overtime. It was a tough game and to be honest, I thought they were going to win.

I've spent more nights at Evan's apartment than my own house the past few weeks, but tonight, I invited Evan over to my place.

I'm not a versatile cook like him, but the few things I know how to cook, I cook well. The doorbell rings as I'm seasoning the steaks. I wipe my hands on a kitchen towel and walk to the door. When I swing it open, Evan is standing there in a pair of tight, black jeans and a lavender polo shirt. It looks gorgeous against his tan skin. We've been out to the small strip of beach several times in the past couple of weeks and Evan is now sporting a delicious dark tan. I shake away the very inappropriate thoughts swirling in my brain. There will be time for that later.

"Come in," I offer, stepping back enough to let him in, but

making sure he has to rub against me as he passes. I take that opportunity to grab his hand as I close the door and pull my very sexy boyfriend in for a kiss.

"You look fucking delicious," I whisper against his ear when I break the kiss.

"Dessert," he promises with a wink, and I consider forgetting the steak, so we can start with dessert. Instead, I adjust myself and lead Evan into the kitchen.

"I opened a bottle of red," I say, handing him a glass of wine. "It will be great with the steak."

"Can I help?"

"You can relax. You cook for me all the time. It's my turn to pamper you tonight. Have a seat." I point to the barstools. "You can keep me company."

Evan sips on his wine while I snap the ends off the asparagus. I've already poked a few holes in the potatoes and put them in the microwave. I walk to the patio with the steaks.

"How do you like yours?" I call to Evan.

"Medium rare to rare. I'm good with a red center."

"Hell, yeah!" I smile. "I was worried you'd want a hockey puck. That might be a deal breaker," I say as he joins me on the patio.

"I can't imagine eating a well-done steak." Evan shudders.

"Me either," I agree, placing the steaks on the grill and setting the timer for five minutes.

Evan follows me back into the kitchen, so I can cook the asparagus. This is my go-to meal when I'm not gorging myself on fast food. It's fast and easy. I need to eat better, but I can't pass up a drive-thru and there are way too many between the stadium and my house. Basically, if it's fast food, I pass it to and from work. One day, it's going to catch up with me.

"Can you go flip the steaks?" I ask Evan when the time beeps.

"Sure." I reset the time for another five minutes when I hear the patio door close as Evan comes back inside.

The microwave dings indicating the potatoes are done. Without asking, Evan walks over and takes them out, piercing each to make sure it's done. About the time I'm taking the asparagus off the stove, the steak timer beeps.

"I'll get them," Evan offers, picking up a clean plate.

By the time he returns with the steaks, I've got everything else on our plates.

"Toppings for the potatoes are on the table. Do you want another glass of wine?"

"Yes, please." Evan picks up both plates and takes them to the table while I pour us wine and grab forks and knives. I appreciate the help. This happens at his house all the time. He insists on cooking for me, but we end up working in together.

"This looks delicious," Evan gushes as I join him at the table.

"It's my favorite meal to cook. I'm not the chef you are, but I do okay with the few things I know how to cook." I ramble on, a little more nervous than I expected to be with Evan in my home.

I like him so much and I want everything to be perfect for him, but I worry that he likes me for reasons other than my sparkling personality. It pisses me off that he's the first guy I've liked since Devante was such an ass to me, and I'm struggling to enjoy our time together because I keep reliving that past relationship.

A small moan from Evan grabs my attention. I smile and raise a brow at him. "You okay?"

"This steak is heaven. It's the best steak I've ever had, and I've had some damn good steaks. What's the seasoning?"

I can't help but beam with pride at his words. "It's my own secret blend." I wink.

"You should package this stuff." He moans again on the next bite. "Wait. You aren't going to tell me what's in it, are you?"

"I told you, it's my *secret* blend." It's so fun to watch the look of horror cross Evan's face. He can't believe I'm not giving up the ingredients. I shrug nonchalantly and take another bite of asparagus, making every effort not to look at him.

"But..." he starts.

"Ple..." he tries again.

"Isa..." he trails off a third time. This time, I glance at him. There's no humor in his eyes. Confusion. Hurt. Shock, but no humor. It cracks me up.

"Why are you laughing at me?" he all but whines.

"Baby, I'm not laughing at you. It's cute to watch you try to figure out what to say. Okay, yeah, I'm laughing at you. I'm also screwing with you. The blend isn't a secret and it's not my creation."

"What? You've been fucking with me this entire time?" A smile slowly appears lighting up his face. "I fell right into that, didn't I?"

"Yep."

"You're proud of yourself." It's not a question and accompanies the sexiest damn smirk.

"Extremely." I wink, rising from the table.

I kiss Evan on the cheek then walk to the counter to grab the bottle of wine and the shaker of steak seasoning. After adding wine to our glasses, I place the seasoning in front of Evan. "This is the best blend on the market. I get it at a specialty shop in Little Havana."

"It's fantastic."

"They have the best fresh produce, a variety of spices, marinades, dressings, and other specialty items that can't be found in most grocery stores."

"We'll have to go one day. I like trying new spices and marinades."

"It's a date!"

Evan's eyes widen slightly then he looks away in an attempt to cover his surprise. I don't call him out on it, but I can't help wondering why he still gets surprised when I mention dates. He's my boyfriend for fucks' sake.

I know he says it doesn't bother him that I want to keep our relationship a secret, but I don't think he's being completely honest about his feelings. Maybe I'm wrong and he doesn't mind keeping us a secret and there's another reason for his shock.

He still won't look at me as he starts clearing the table and washing the dishes. Now the silence between has grown uncomfortable. Where did the night go wrong?

"Hey," I say, taking the plate from him and setting it in the sink. I pick up the dish towel and dry his hands then pull him against my chest. He stiffens in my arms. "What's wrong?" I ask, gently stroking his back.

"Nothing." He tries to pull away, but I hold him in place while continuing to rub his back.

"You can tell me. I lo..." The word gets caught in my throat. It's too soon. We've only been dating a few weeks. Hell, Evan might not feel what I'm feeling, but I've thought those words a hundred times or more in the past couple of weeks. *Tell him how you feel,* I silently encourage myself. Taking a small step back to put enough space between us so I can look Evan in the eye, I cup his face in my hands.

"I love you, Evan." His breath hitches and unshed tears sting his eyes. He starts to shake his head. "It's true. I love you. It might seem fast, but I know how I feel," I tell him honestly.

"Isaac, I..." he trails off, looking everywhere but at me.

"It's okay if you're not there yet." It cuts like a fucking knife, but I don't want him to say something he doesn't mean or isn't ready to admit.

"It's not that," he whispers. "I've felt the same way since our first date."

I wait several seconds, maybe even a minute for him to continue, but he doesn't say more.

"Talk to me," I all but beg.

"Why?" It's one simple word with too many possible answers.

"Why what?"

"Why do you love me?"

"What? How can I not love you. You're funny, smart, honest, selfless, nice, fun to be around, and sexy as hell."

"No. I'm not those things."

"You are and so much more."

I had no idea Evan believed so little in himself. When we tried to have sex a few weeks ago, he freaked out a little. Now I'm wondering if there is more to the story about his ex than he shared with me. I take his hand and lead him to the couch. Cleaning the kitchen can wait. I sit down first then pull Evan down next to me scooting him against my side and wrapping my arms around him.

"Does this have anything to do with your last relationship?"

He tenses in my arms, telling me my guess is right. "It was bad."

"Do you want to talk about it?"

"I doubt you want to hear what a shit boyfriend I was or how I'll never measure up."

"Measure up to what?"

"Whatever expectations you have for me."

"Evan, I expect you to be exactly who you are. I love you, the Evan I ran into in August, the Evan I took to the beach on our first date, not some version of you I've created in my head. I want you."

"That's hard for me to believe. Mike told me who to be and every time I thought I was measuring up to his expectations, he'd change his mind and want a different version of me. It was a constant rollercoaster of being the person he told me to be and then failing in his eyes and switching again."

"That sounds miserable."

"It was a shitty two years, but I stayed because I didn't think I deserved anyone better."

"*He* didn't think you deserved better."

"Basically. And he convinced me I wasn't good enough for anyone else and he was doing me a favor by dating me."

"That's seriously messed up."

"I'm pretty sure he was cheating on me. We hadn't had sex in more than nine months before we broke up. At first, he made up excuses, but when I got up the nerve to confront him, he said I was terrible in bed, and he couldn't stand to be with me. Like an idiot, I stayed for months. Sadly, if I hadn't taken this job, we'd probably still be together."

"Damn, Evan. That's awful." Now I'm pissed. I'd like to meet this Mike guy and beat the shit out of him. "No one deserves to be treated that way. You are an amazing person. I'm sorry he did those things to you."

"It's my own fault. I knew he was a crappy boyfriend from the beginning but felt like he was the best I could do, so I stuck around and allowed him to treat me like crap."

"Not to be overly confident, but I'd say you definitely upgraded." Evan laughs at my words.

"Conceited much?"

"Confident," I correct.

"Keep telling yourself that." Evan sighs heavily and snuggles closer to me. "You're right. I upgraded quite a bit. Isaac," Evan says, pushing himself up so he can look at my face. "I love you, too." Then his lips are on mine. We kiss for several minutes before he scoots back and runs his hand along my jawline. "Thank you."

"For what?" I inquire.

"For being a great man. For having the confidence to tell me how you feel. For listening to me talk about my past. For making me feel safe and loved and giving me the encouragement to tell you what I've been thinking for weeks. I. Love. You."

SEVENTEEN
EVAN

 Last night took its toll on me and today, I'm exhausted. After the heart to heart with Isaac, he invited me to spend the night. We still haven't had sex, but the foreplay is definitely moving in that direction and it's getting harder to stop. Part of me is ready to take that next step with Isaac, but a bigger part is worried about how he'll react. I wasn't lying when I told him I don't have much experience. Other than my college boyfriend and a couple of one-night stands, Mike is the only other person I've slept with and he tore me down to the point where I'm not sure I'll ever be whole again.

Isaac is patient and says he's fine with taking things as slowly as I want. Mike would say similar things then rip me apart when he changed his mind. Every time I put Isaac off, I wait for him to get mad and tell me he's had enough of my crap.

It doesn't help my self-confidence to know I'm keeping a big secret from Isaac. If it ever comes out, it will be the end of us. No matter what, I have to keep my ever-mounting debt from him.

"Good morning," Hope calls from the other room when she arrives thirty minutes earlier than her eight-thirty start time. I've already been here an hour. I couldn't sleep so I got up early, left Isaac a note, and rushed home to shower and change. There was no reason to sit around the house waiting to begin my day, so I came in early.

"Good morning," I respond, walking into the larger room. "You're early."

"I have to leave a little early today for that appointment."

"Oh, yes, sorry, I forgot."

"It's fine. Here, I brought us a treat from the new bakery down the street." Hope hands me a coffee and a small, white bag.

"Thank you. What do I owe you?"

"Nothing. My treat. Enjoy."

I open the bag and see a cherry Danish. One of my favorites. "I appreciate it. This looks and smells wonderful."

"I ate my Danish in the car. It was divine. I considered eating yours, too," she admits.

"Hey, no backsies," I tease, hugging the bag close to me.

"You're a mess," she laughs.

My phone dings with a text, so I set the bag on the edge of Hope's desk and dig out my phone. Not even technically at work and I'm already getting texts. When I slide my phone open, I see Isaac's name instead of an employee needing something. I don't even try to hide my smile as my heart races.

Isaac: Good morning, Sexy. I missed waking up next to you.

Isaac: Thank you for the sweet note.

Me: Good morning. Sorry I bailed. I couldn't sleep.

Isaac: Are you okay?

Me: Yeah. Last night was... a lot.

Isaac: It did get a little heavy.

Isaac: We balanced the stressful conversation with a little... FUN!

Me: FUN is an understatement.

What we did was make out like a couple of horny teenagers. It was more than fun. It was exciting, hot, sexy, and better than any make out session I've experienced. It was hard to leave the warmth and safety of Isaac's bed this morning, but part of me was hesitant to face him. I know he isn't anything like Mike, but a small part of me still fears he will reject me or tell me how boring I am in bed.

Isaac: It was sexy as fuck, and I can't wait to do it again... and more.

Isaac: When you're ready. No pressure.

Every time he says things like that another brick falls from the wall I've created. I believe him. I trust him. Standing there, staring at my phone, I realize for the first time, I truly believe those thoughts. I do trust Isaac and I believe he loves me.

Isaac: I have to be at the airport early Saturday afternoon to leave for our away game. I'd like to take you out Friday since we won't see each other for a couple of days.

Isaac: I know it's still a few days away, but I need to make a reservation and want to make sure you're available.

Me: I'd like that.

Isaac: Good. I've been wanting to take you to my favorite place. Can you meet me at my house around seven? We can take one car and then you can spend the night.

Me: It's a date!

I add a few heart emojis.

Isaac: Have a good day. I love you.

Me: You, too. I love you.

When I finally pocket my phone and look up, Hope is staring at me with a knowing look on her face. Without a word, I pick up my bag and coffee, turning for my office. Three steps later, Hope speaks.

"Not so fast. That was quite a smile. Something you want to share?"

"Nothing to share," I lie.

She scoffs, "Right. Look, I tend to play mama bear to Carter and his friends, so I'm just going to come right out with it. Was that Isaac?"

"Wh-what? Why would you ask me that?" Not only do I sound completely unconvincing, but I don't even bother turning around to look at Hope. How does she know about us? This is bad. This is really bad.

"He's a great guy. You two make a cute couple."

"No. It's not like that. We're friends." I'm sure she can hear the terror in my voice.

"Evan, is everything alright?" she asks, coming to stand in

front of me. If she didn't hear the fear, she can see it on my face and her demeanor changes. "Hey, what's wrong? If I'm wrong about you two, tell me. I thought I picked up on a vibe between you when we were setting up the office. He's stopped by the office a few times and I've seen you two talking in the hallway."

"Is it obvious?"

"Kind of."

"Shit." I drop into the nearest chair and set my breakfast on the desk next to it. "You can't tell anyone what you think you know."

"You mean what I *know* I know," she teases.

"Hope, please," I beg.

She pulls over a chair and sits, facing me. "What's going on, Evan?"

"I can't tell you."

"You can't tell me that you and Isaac are dating?"

"Shhh." I frantically look around the office to make sure no one else has walked in and overhead our conversation. "Please. It's a secret. No one can know. No. One."

"Okay. I won't tell anyone. I'm sorry if I put you in an awkward position. I think you guys are perfect for each other."

"I think so, too, but..." I trail off, not wanting to tell her Isaac's private business.

"Isaac isn't out," she finishes for me. I nod. "Don't worry. I'll keep it to myself."

"Thank you."

Hope returns to her desk, and I go into my office, closing the door behind me. I hate having the door closed, but I need a few minutes to compose myself. What the hell am I going to do? I can't tell Isaac that Hope knows. Can I? Should I? Great. One more secret to add to the list. Boyfriend of the Year.

EIGHTEEN
ISAAC

The doorbell rings a little before seven. I've been pacing the kitchen for the past fifteen minutes. Taking Evan to Francisco's sounded like a good idea on Tuesday morning, but now I'm having second thoughts. It's the perfect place for a date night if I want the world to know about Evan and me. The atmosphere is romantic and it's becoming more and more difficult to keep my hands off the man I love. I'm afraid this secret is going to ruin us.

"Hey," I greet with a smile I hope masks my inner turmoil.

"Hello."

Evan follows me into the house. "Do you want a glass of wine or a beer before we leave?"

"Sure. Red wine if you have it."

I pour us both a glass and hand one to Evan. For two people who rarely drank before we met, it's becoming part of every date now. It's usually only a glass or two, but definitely a change from the norm.

"This is good. It's different than the one we had with the steaks."

"Yeah, that was a Pinot Noir. This is a Malbec."

"I like it."

"I thought I'd call for a car so I can buy my boyfriend a bottle of wine at my favorite restaurant." I lean in and kiss him for several seconds before breaking the kiss and picking up my phone from the counter. "I made a reservation for seven forty-five, so I'll go ahead and call the car while we enjoy our wine."

I pull up my app and once I secure a car, I lead Evan to the couch. "How was your day?" I ask but start kissing him again before he can answer. When he breaks the kiss, I chuckle. "Sorry. I can't get enough of you."

"I'm okay with that." He winks and takes a sip of his wine. "To answer your question, my day was good. How was practice?"

"Not bad. My workout this morning was more intense than practice." I stare at Evan and his pupils darken at my implication.

"Intense? Why?" he croaks, his voice coming out a little higher than normal.

I clear my throat and take a sip of my wine. We're not going to make it to dinner at this rate. "Let's just say, I was a little worked up this morning even after a cold shower and taking care of... things."

I stayed at Evan's last night and we got a little hot and heavy this morning before I left for practice. It was the best *not sex* I've had. It's getting more and more difficult to stop myself. I'm not going to push Evan to do something he's not ready for, but I need him more than I've ever needed anyone.

Evan scoots closer and runs a hand from my knee to my crotch at an agonizingly slow pace. Anticipation rocks me and fire shoots through me when he rubs my hardening cock. "What kind of things?" he whispers.

My heart beats faster and my breath is heavy. Closing my eyes, I drop my head to the back of the couch. "You know what kind of things," I barely get out.

My phone dings, alerting me the car is here. Fuck! Evan moves his hand, stands up, downs the rest of his wine all in one fluid motion as if he didn't work me up to the point that a few more seconds would have made me need a change of clothes.

"Let's go," he calls, opening the door while I remain motionless on the couch. It takes another couple of minutes before I calm down enough to join him.

"You'll pay for that," I whisper as I lock the door. It's a promise I made last Sunday, but never followed through on. This time, he's not going to get away with it.

Once we're settled in the back seat of the car, I feel more like myself. The restaurant is only a ten-minute drive, so we should arrive about five minutes early.

"Can I ask you a question, man?" the driver asks, looking at me through the rearview mirror.

"Sure," I respond. This isn't an unusual request. Actually, it is. Most people aren't this respectful before invading my personal life.

"Are you Isaac Flores?"

"Yes." No reason to lie. It will come back to bite me later.

"Cool. You played a damn good game last week. Three touchdowns. Awesome."

"Thanks. Were you at the game?"

"I wish. I watched it at one of the bars near the stadium and then drove drunk fans home for two hours." I don't say anything else. I'm not sure how to respond to that. When I don't say anything, he continues. "Guys' night out or meeting a couple of hot dates?"

"Guys' night out," I answer absently.

"Nice. I bet you two will have hot chicks hanging all over you tonight."

"Maybe."

He snorts. "Maybe, my ass. Famous people get all the bitches. It unfair to rest of the population."

Thankfully, we pull up in front of the restaurant and this ridiculous conversation ends. I add a tip to the app and thank him for the ride.

"Good evening, sir, do you have a reservation?" the hostess asks when we walk inside.

"Yes, Flores for two."

She picks up a couple of menus, "Right this way, gentleman." She leads us to a table near the back. It's enough out of the way that we won't have people gawking at us if they recognize me, but not so secluded that it's private or appears to outsiders that we're on a romantic date. The more time I spend with Evan, the more I hate feeling I need to keep us a secret. It's hard not to hold his hand every time I'm near him.

"Your waitress will be right with you," the hostess states while handing us each a menu and a list of specials.

"Thank you," Evan and I say at the same time.

Evan looks over the menu and I can't help but watch him. He's in awe. Francisco's is impressive from the expensive, wooden features, gold-etched fixtures, and white-linen table-cloths to the impressive wine list and variety of dinner and dessert options.

"They are known for their steaks and seafood, but everything is delicious, especially their desserts."

"How can I possibly choose?"

"I'm getting the bluefin tuna. It pairs well with their

signature pinot noir," I tell him, referring to the list of Francisco's wine. The owners also have a winery in France.

"I'm thinking about getting this blue-cheese-encrusted filet."

"It's phenomenal and will go well with the pinot. If you're interested, I'll order us a bottle."

"That sounds perfect. I want to taste your tuna if you don't mind," he sounds skeptical like he shouldn't have asked for a taste of my food.

"Bite for a bite," I agree.

"What?"

"It's something we did as a family when I was a kid. We couldn't afford to eat out often, so when we did, it was a treat. All five of us would order something different and trade a bite for a bite with each other so we could taste all the dishes."

"Bite for a bite," he repeats. "I like it. Deal."

After we order and have our bottle of wine, we fall into easy conversation. Evan is completely relaxed and seems genuinely happy. It's nice to see him this way. I was worried about him after he told me about his asshole ex earlier this week. I'd like to get my hands on that jerk. How can anyone treat Evan that way? He's a wonderful man and deserves to be treated like a prince or maybe a king.

"Oh, hey, I forgot to tell you, my parents are coming to visit in a few days. They called this morning and surprised me with the news. They'll arrive on Wednesday and leave on Saturday."

"Why aren't they staying for the game?"

"They aren't big football fans. They've been to a couple of games over the years, but it's not their thing. I understand. Honestly, I didn't care much for it until I started working at the stadium. Actually, I worked at the stadium in Rutherford for three years before I even watched a game on TV."

"Are you kidding?"

"Nope. It just wasn't something we did. Now, I love it."

"Can you take any time off while they're here?"

"Their plane doesn't get in until after eight on Wednesday night, so I'm going to send a car to pick them up at the airport and bring them to the stadium. That way I can work late. Then I'm taking off Thursday and Friday, but I'll be available if something major comes up that Hope can't handle."

"Good. I'm glad you can spend time with them."

"Do you want to meet them? It's fine if you're not ready. I hate not to see you for three days, but I know you're not comfortable telling people about..." he trails off, waving his hand between us.

I sit back in my chair and take a long sip from my glass of wine.

"I would love to meet them, but I'm not sure I'm ready for them to know about us." Evan's face drops. Damn. The last thing I want to do is hurt him. I should have chosen my words more carefully.

"Okay," he speaks barely above a whisper.

"Evan, please understand. What if they tell someone?"

"They won't."

"I'm sure they won't, but I... I'm... scared."

"I know you are, and I respect how you feel. We don't have to tell them, but I can't promise my mom won't figure it out."

"Can I think about it?"

"Of course."

The rest of dinner is only slightly awkward. *Good job, Isaac. Way to ruin a perfect evening. You need to get over yourself or you're going to lose the best thing that's ever happened to you,* I silently chastise myself.

An hour later, we're back home, relaxing on the couch

with another glass of wine. I've had too much and I'm going to regret it in the morning. I rarely have this many drinks in one night even during the off season.

Evan is still on edge, and I don't how to change the course of our night. I'm afraid he's going to choose to go home. More than anything, I need him in my bed tonight. I need to know we're okay. I can handle another night without sex. Hell, we don't even have to kiss as long as he snuggles close, and I can hold him in my arms.

Without a word, Evan takes my glass and sets it on the table next to his. He shocks me when he straddles me. He slides one hand along my jaw then follows it with small kisses. Instead of kissing my lips, he continues peppering kisses down my neck then up to my ear, tangling one hand in my hair. I wrap my hands around him, pulling him closer. He crashes his lips against mine, pushing his tongue into my mouth, his kiss is urgent and needy. He pulls back long enough to take off my shirt then his own before his mouth is on mine again. He pushes against me, and the contact sends shock waves rolling through me.

"I want you," he mumbles against my lips. It takes a second for my brain to function and process his words. My eyes go wide. Before I have a chance to respond, he rasps, "Take me."

With those words, I stand up and Evan wraps his legs around me. I carry him to my bed and drop him onto the soft mattress, hovering over him.

"Are you sure?"

"Yes. I need you inside me. I love you, Isaac, and I can't wait another minute to make love to you."

I stand up long enough to take the rest of my clothes off and grab the lube and a condom from the dresser. When I turn back to Evan, he's naked and on his back a little further up on the bed.

"Gorgeous," I growl. I toss the lube and condom on the bed and kneel between his legs, leaning down to kiss him. Slowly, I lick down his chest over one nipple, sucking on it then the other before making my way down to his tip. I lick the drop of pre-cum and harden more at the sound that escapes Evan, a sound somewhere between pleasure and pain. I get it. My dick is painfully hard right now. Sitting back, I squeeze lube on my fingers and carefully work one into Evan.

"Oh, god," he moans.

"Told you, you'd call me god," I tease. His eyes darken and a smile plays at his lips, but it turns into another moan when I push a second finger inside.

"Please," he begs. "I need you. Now."

I roll on the condom and coat my sheathed dick with lube. I never take my eyes off Evan's as I slowly push inside, giving him time to adjust and me a minute to get my composure.

"Move. Please." His words come out gravelly and barely audible. When I don't move, Evan grabs my ass and pulls me deeper into him. I lean down and kiss him before pulling out a little and slamming into him.

"Fuck, yeah," he groans.

Need takes over and I start moving, slow at first, but every noise Evan makes goes straight to my dick, causing me to move faster and faster. He reaches down to stroke himself, but I push his hand away, grabbing both his wrists and pinning him to the bed. Plowing into him harder and harder until I blow my load into the condom much too soon.

"Fuck. That. Was. Hot," Evan gasps between breaths. I pull out of him and scoot down the bed enough to take him in my mouth. "Shit. Isaac. God that feels amazing."

I move my mouth up and down his shaft several times, working him deeper into my throat. After several minutes, he taps my shoulder. I don't bother stopping. He taps me again.

"Isaac, I'm gonna..." Without finishing the thought, he releases into my mouth. I swallow every drop, slowly releasing him and falling down beside him.

"That was perfect. Holy shit, you're good," I tell him. He smiles at me, wrapping an arm around me and pulling the comforter over us. Home. This is where I belong. "I love you, Evan."

He responds with a quiet snore. I wore my baby out.

NINETEEN
EVAN

 My parents arrived last night, and we had a late dinner before going to bed. We were all too tired to spend any real time together. This morning, I took them out for breakfast and showed them around a little.

I gave them a tour of the stadium and we watched the team practice for about thirty minutes. They were impressed with the employee box and even commented that they might come for a game later in the season.

Even though I know my employees should be good for the next few days without me, it makes me nervous being away. I'm somewhat of a workaholic and control freak. I like to do everything myself rather than rely on others to help. Hope knows to call if something comes up she can't handle. Ha, as if that will happen. She can probably do my job better than me. It will do me good to keep that in mind and enjoy this time with my parents. I'd never been away from them for more than a few days before moving to Miami three months ago.

Three months. Wow. It's hard to believe I haven't lived here longer. I finally found my rhythm at work, making the job less stressful, and I've fallen in love with my perfect man.

"What are you doing out here?" Mom asks, joining me on the small balcony. She and Dad laid down for a quick nap after lunch.

"Thinking."

"Anything you want to share."

"Thinking about how much I'm enjoying Miami. I wasn't sure the first few weeks if I would like living here. I missed home and you guys so much, but I've made some friends and I love my job."

"Have you met anyone special?"

"What? Why would ask me that?" My voice is a little high, likely giving away my lie.

"Because you're different. You're happier than I've ever seen you and I'm wondering if that has something to do with a man."

"You're getting ahead of yourself," I assert.

"You'll tell me about him when you're ready," she declares, patting my leg. "As long as he treats you well. You don't need a repeat of Mike.

How the hell do moms always know your business even when you say absolutely nothing to give anything away? It's like some weird mom superpower. If this conversation continues, I'm going to slip up and give my relationship with Isaac away. I have to respect his wishes and keep the secret whether I agree with him or not.

"I assure you, I will never let anyone treat me the way Mike did." I give her a little reassurance without giving anything away. "How about a glass of wine?" I offer. Mom enjoys sweet, white wine, so I bought a few bottles of her favorite Moscato.

"That sounds nice."

"Relax. I'll bring it to you."

When I get to the kitchen, Dad is there drinking a glass of water.

"Hey, Dad. Would you like to join Mom and me on the balcony for a drink?"

"Sure. Can I help with anything?"

"Yeah, you can bring Mom her wine," I tell him as I fill a glass for her. "What do you want? I have bourbon, this Moscato, and a bottle of red."

"Red, please."

After opening the bottle and pouring him a glass, Dad takes the drinks outside while I prepare some snacks, filling a platter with cheese, crackers, nuts, and apple slices. I'm on my way outside when my phone dings with a text, so I set the platter on the table and check my phone in case it's work.

> Isaac: I miss you. Having fun with your parents?

> Me: Yeah, it's been nice catching up. I took them to Little Havana today and we're going to the beach tomorrow.

> Me: I miss you, too.

> Isaac: I'm sorry I can't be there.

> Me: It's okay.

Is it really okay? I'm not completely convinced, but I'm trying to understand. It was easy in the beginning when I didn't know him very well. Now that we've moved further along in the relationship and professed our love to each other, it's getting harder. I want to tell everyone Isaac Flores is my boyfriend, not because he's famous and I want the status. On the contrary, I have no desire to be the next headline. I want everyone to know how much I love this man and how lucky I am to have him in my life.

Isaac: Thank you for understanding.

Me: I love you.

Isaac: I love you.

I shove my phone back into my pocket and join my parents on the balcony. The weather is beautiful today–seventy-five with a light breeze. It's comfortable enough to sit outside without sweating and being miserable.

After a couple of bourbons and remembering the encouragement Isaac gave me when we discussed the topic, I get up the nerve to ask the question that's been bothering me for most of my life.

I clear my throat and blurt out, "Can I ask you guys a question?" It comes out a little more aggressively than I meant for it to and both my parents look at me with concern.

"Of course, sweetie. You can ask us anything," Mom tells me.

"Did you want me?"

"What? Evan, why would you ask us that? Of course, we wanted you."

"I'm sorry. I didn't mean for it come out quite like that. I know you love me, but why did you wait almost ten years to have me? Was I an accident?"

"How long has this been worrying you?" Mom asks.

"Since I was a kid," I admit with a shrug.

Mom and Dad share a look, then Mom takes my hand, "We were very young when we married. Our parents were against it for that reason and did not help us at all. It was hard the first few years trying to make ends meet. We were both working two jobs and trying to take college classes. We wanted a baby but knew we couldn't afford to have one. When we were twenty-four, we both graduated from college. It took a little longer for us since we couldn't go full-time. We started trying as soon as we both got a good job. We lost the first two babies, and the doctor encouraged us not to try again, but we refused to listen. When I got pregnant with you, we were elated, but terrified. We didn't tell anyone, even our parents, until I was twenty weeks. I didn't have any issues with the pregnancy or birth. After you were born, we decided to be grateful for our one perfect child and not try again."

"I'm sorry. I didn't mean to bring up painful memories."

"You didn't. We lost the babies very early in my pregnancy. It didn't make the loss easy, but we have you and don't dwell on what we lost."

"Did you want a big family?"

"Not really," Dad answers. "We talked about having two children, but always said we'd be happy with one."

"Thank you for sharing that with me."

"You can ask us anything. We will always be honest with you."

And now I feel guilty for keeping secrets from them, one I want to tell them so much. I can't wait until I can share Isaac with them. The other one, I'm happy to keep to myself. No one needs to know about my debt.

TWENTY
ISAAC

 A knock on the door startles me and I almost fall off the couch where I was just about asleep. I don't know why I'm so tired. With Evan's parents in town, I've been going to bed early. It takes me a minute to get my bearings and stretch out my sore muscles. The knock sounds again, reminding me there's a reason I'm awake now.

When I open the door, I'm met with a sexy as hell, Evan, wearing a pair of white dress pants and a white linen jacket that's open. He's not wearing a shirt and his tan skin looks delicious against the white fabric. My cock hardens at the sight of my beautiful man.

"My parents left for the airport an hour ago, so I decided to bring you a present." He smiles, holding his arms out.

I pull him into my house and growl in his ear, "The gift better be you." As soon as my mouth crashes onto his, I wrap my arms around Evan and he tangles his hands in my hair. Need takes over, hands are everywhere, and we can't get enough of each other. It's only been three days, but I feel like

I haven't had Evan's touch in months. I need him now. He pulls on the hem of my shirt, so I raise my arms for him to pull it off. His jacket hits the floor next. By the time we make our way down the hall to my bedroom, we're both naked and a trail of clothes lies in our wake.

Evan takes over, pushing me onto the bed, trailing kisses down my chest, stopping before he reaches my cock. He sits back and pushes my legs up before leaning down and licking my aching hole.

"Fuck," I gasp. "Do that again." No one has ever licked my ass before. Shit, it feels amazing. Evan slowly runs his tongue over my hole several more times, driving me mad. My breath comes out fast and heavy. I can't focus. Holy crap, I'm going to come if he doesn't stop soon. I try to tell him, but I can't form a complete thought much less speak.

Suddenly, Evan sits up, smiling down at me, "Feel good?"

All I can do is nod and smile. I didn't even come and I'm flying higher than ever. Damn, he's good at that. A cold touch has me jumping and focusing back on Evan's face.

"Relax," he whispers, "I've got you." He slowly pushes one lubed finger into me then a second, working his fingers to prepare me for his cock. He pulls his fingers out, rolls a condom on, and slowly pushes himself into me. A slight sting shoots through me and I gasp. Evan freezes.

"Are you okay?"

"Perfect. Move. Now." I grab Evan's ass and pull him into me. He leans down and kisses me then starts pounding into me, hard and fast. "Yes. Oh, fuck. Yes."

The more I moan and talk, the harder Evan fucks me. Damn he feels good. His fingers dig into my sides as he pounds me harder and harder. Reaching down, I grab my own cock, using my precum to coat it. Three pulls and I explode all over my stomach and chest. Evan's release follows. He collapses onto my chest, breathing heavily.

"That. Was. Awesome," he rasps out. When his breathing slows, he carefully pulls out of me and walks to the bathroom. He returns with a warm, damp cloth and wipes my come off my chest then wipes the cloth over my used hole. It's a sweet gesture. No one has ever cleaned me up after sex. Evan walks back to the bathroom and after cleaning himself, he crawls into the bed next to me and snuggles close.

"Thank you for taking care of me. I've never done that before," I admit.

Evan bolts up, "What?"

Suddenly shy, I avert my eyes. "Nothing."

"It's okay, Isaac. What do you mean?"

"I've never had a guy lick my ass or fuck me. I'm always the top."

"Oh, I'm sorry. You should have told me. We didn't have to... I thought it was... Mike always made me do those things to him," Evan admits barely above a whisper.

Rage courses through me. In the calmest voice I can muster, I ask, "What do you mean he *made* you do those things?" If that bastard forced Evan to do anything, I might hunt him down.

"He made me rim him. I fucking hated it. I did it tonight because he told me that's what good boyfriends do. I didn't know I had a choice."

"You always have a choice with me. I never want you to do something you don't like. You don't have to do it ever again."

Slowly, a smile spreads across Evan's face, "Actually, I want to do it again. I loved doing it to you."

"Are you sure?"

"Yeah. Did you like it?"

"It was absolutely fucking amazing. Some of the best sex I've ever had. I didn't know it could feel that good. Hell, I didn't know I was a vers."

Evan's demeanor changes and the tension from a few minutes ago fades away. "You are now," Evan teases, laying back down and cuddling against me.

With my arms wrapped around him we both start to fall asleep. I want to ask him more about his visit with his parents and I'm starting to get hungry, but right now, I need to hold my boyfriend and revel in this newfound interest. I will definitely be letting Evan take control in bed again.

When I open my eyes, I'm surprised to find it dark in the room and the bed cold next to me. Where is Evan? I push myself up and blink a few times letting my eyes adjust. I have no idea what time it is or where I left my phone when things got hot and heavy. I wince at the slight, but oh, so delicious, sting in my ass as I climb out of bed. It's the best feeling–a small reminder of the mind-blowing sex we had.

I stumble to the bathroom to take care of some business then pull on a clean pair of boxer briefs. The hallway light is off, and the house is quiet. When I get to the kitchen, a quick glance at the microwave tells me it's a little after eight. The lights are on in the backyard and there's an open bottle of red wine and a clean glass on the counter. I pour myself a glass and take it to the backyard where I find Evan, sipping his own wine and reading a book.

"Hey," I smile when he looks up at me, "did you enjoy your nap?"

"It was great. Sorry I fell asleep for so long," I apologize.

"Someone wore you out." He smirks.

"You definitely did and in the best way possible." I kiss his cheek then drop onto the small couch next to him. He's wearing a pair of black sweatpants and a solid red shirt. He came prepared. "How long have you been awake?"

"About two hours. I only napped for thirty minutes. I couldn't fall back asleep, so I borrowed your key and went home to shower and change then came back with an overnight bag and some dinner. You were still asleep, so I made a snack and came out here to read. It's a gorgeous night and the breeze feels great."

"You should have woken me."

"I tried. You didn't budge, so I figured you needed the rest."

"What are you reading?"

"It's a murder mystery I picked up when I was out with my parents yesterday. I started reading it on the beach. It's really good. Lots of twists and turns."

"Sounds good. Maybe I'll read it after you finish. I'm not much of a reader. I always enjoy it, but I never think to grab a book instead of watching mindless television."

"I've always been a big reader, but I haven't read much since moving here."

"We should go to the bookstore soon and pick something out we both might like."

"It's a date! You enjoy that glass of wine. I'm going to go get our dinner. Help yourself to the snacks," Evan says, rising from the couch and pointing to the plate of cheese and grapes."

"Can I help you?" I offer.

"No, thank you. I want to do this for you. It will only take a few minutes." Evan disappears into the house, so I pick up his book and read it while he busies himself with dinner.

TWENTY-ONE
EVAN

The visit with my parents last weekend was great and I was sad to see them go, but the time with Isaac after they left was nothing short of perfection. Once I got past the initial shock of doing something to him that he had never experienced and got Mike out of my head, I felt damn proud of myself for teaching Isaac something new.

We've spent every night this week together and sometimes I wonder why we pay for two places. I'm not ready to bring that up to Isaac yet. We've only been together about six weeks.

Today, Isaac leaves for another away game and then next week, his family will be here.

Normally, I don't come into the office on Saturday when the boys are away, but there's a huge concert at the stadium tonight, so we need all hands on deck. Hope is here, too, and Isaac promised to stop by before the team leaves for the airport.

Carter walks in followed by Tyson and Isaac. It's not quite the goodbye I was hoping for. Isaac isn't going to kiss me with an audience. Good thing I took care of my boyfriend last night and again this morning.

Isaac speaks to Hope then walks over to me while Carter and Tyson talk to her. All I want to do is jump into his arms, but I stay glued to my spot and wait for him to approach. Keeping my features unreadable is almost impossible, but I will do anything for Isaac even if it means pretending he's just a friend.

"I'm going to miss you," he whispers, so no one else can hear.

"Me, too," I choke out. It worries me every time he gets on a plane. I know the chances of something terrible happening are slim, but I worry until I get the text telling me they landed safely.

"Thank you for that amazing sendoff this morning." He winks and shows me his sexiest smirk. Damn, him. All I can do is nod. Words refuse to form, so I stare deep into his dark-brown eyes.

"Isaac," Tyson calls, breaking the trance. "Let's go."

"I'll be right there," Isaac growls.

I glance over his shoulder and see Tyson shake his head as he whispers something to Carter. They both laugh then leave the office.

"You better go," I tell him.

"The bus won't leave me."

I laugh at his confidence. The bus might not leave him, but the coaches are going to have his ass if he holds them up.

"See ya," he says with one more wink then turns to Hope. "Have a good weekend."

"You two make such a cute couple." Hope's eyes go wide as soon as the words leave her mouth. Isaac freezes a few steps from the door and my stomach drops. Shit. Fuck. Damn. This is bad. Really bad. Worse than when she called me out a couple of weeks ago.

"What did you say?" Isaac asks in an eerily calm voice. His face is full of anger and rage, but his words quiet.

"Nothing. I'm sorry. Evan told me not to say anything. It slipped out," she falls all over her words, trying to smooth it over, but only making it worse.

"Hope—," I start, but Isaac cuts me off.

"You told her. You know how important it is to me for this," he points between us, "to be kept between us and you fucking told her. Then had the audacity to tell her to lie to me."

"That's not what happened, Isaac." I take a step toward him, but he takes three steps back.

"You're a liar and a gossip."

"It's not gossip, and I didn't lie about anything." Tears burn my eyes. "Isaac, please listen."

"No!" he barks. He shakes his head and rushes out the door.

I run after him, but when I reach the hallway, he's already disappeared around the corner. I walk into my office and close the door, not bothering to acknowledge Hope when she tries to talk to me.

She shouldn't have let it slip out, but Isaac's reaction is not her fault. That doesn't matter to me right now. All that matters is I might have lost the best thing that's ever happened to me.

Even if Isaac is willing to speak to me, it will be Monday after work before I see him. By then, he will have had plenty of time to decide I'm not worth the hassle. He asked me to do one thing and I failed him.

It's going to be a long, lonely weekend.

TWENTY-TWO
ISAAC

"Let's talk," Tyson insists, falling in step next to me as we walk to our cars Monday afternoon. Carter flanks me on the opposite side. What the hell is this?

"About what?" I growl. I'm not in the mood for him. I want to go home and wallow in my misery. Evan did the one thing I asked him not to do. I don't know if I'll ever be able to forgive him.

"Get in," he commands when we reach his car. Carter climbs in the backseat and Tyson raises an eyebrow at me, motioning for me to get in the car. I don't know what this is about, but I guess I'm going to find out.

Tyson drives in silence to a secluded bar and grill about five miles from the stadium. It won't be crowded at three on a Monday afternoon. I follow him and Carter inside and to a table in the back. The waitress follows us with some menus. Tyson orders three beers for us. As soon as the girl is out of earshot, he looks at me.

"Start talking," Tyson commands.

"About what? I have no idea what this is about."

"For starters, you've been an asshole since we stopped by my mom's office on Saturday. My guess is you had a fight with your boyfriend," Carter states. I stand up, knocking my chair over and stalk toward the door. "Bingo," I hear Carter say.

I turn on my heels and rush back to the table, leaning down, getting in Carter's face. He doesn't even flinch. Cocky bastard.

"I don't know what you think you know or what the hell Hope told you, but my private life is none of your damn business and it will do you well to stay the fuck out of it and keep your mouth shut."

"Sit the fuck down, Isaac!" Tyson snaps, picking up the chair and setting it behind me. His voice gives no room for argument. I don't want to have this conversation with them, but I reluctantly drop into the chair and rest my head in my hands.

My friends are quiet for a minute as I hear the waitress approaching. "Here you go, gentlemen. Can I get you anything else?"

"Not right now. Thank you," Tyson replies. A few seconds later, he continues talking to me. "Look. Clearly, something is going on with you. We're your friends, Isaac. You can talk to us."

"It's nothing. I'm fine."

"Well, playing like shit, being a complete jerk all weekend, and getting injured for being stupid on the field tells a different story."

He's right. I let this shit show with Evan get in my head and took it out on my teammates and on the other team. It got me injured and taken out of the game in the third quarter. In my head, I was convinced I could still play, and it pissed me off Coach sequestered me to the bench. It was the right call. I won't be on the field for a few weeks now and if he had let me play, I probably would have done something else stupid or gotten a more serious injury.

I take a long drink from my beer, trying to decide what exactly I want to say to my two closest friends. At some point, I have to stop lying about who I am, no matter the cost, but I have to be ready to pay the price.

"What do you know?" I take the chickenshit way out.

"We don't know anything. We guess there is something between you and Evan," Tyson says.

"Why do you think that?"

Carter laughs beside me, "It's obvious. Every time I go see my mom, you tag along. You never did that when Sandy was her boss. When the two of you are in the same room, you can't take your eyes off each other."

"So, no one told you anything about us."

"No. Who would tell us?" Tyson asks.

"Hope. Evan."

"You told my mom, but not us. Wow, some friend." Carter holds his chest as if I've shot an arrow straight through it. Dramatic ass.

"I didn't tell anyone. It is supposed to be a secret."

"You do a crap job of keeping it a secret," Tyson deadpans.

"Am I really that obvious?"

"Yes!" They both say at the same time.

I shake my head. No use keeping it from them now. "Well, you've figured out that I'm gay," I say to Carter, since Tyson already knows that part. "You might as well know, I've been dating Evan since the day after we met. We went on a date, and I knew immediately. We've been keeping it a secret because I don't want the media to get ahold of the story. It's no one's business."

"That doesn't explain why you've been such an ass," Carter replies.

"He told Hope after I asked him to keep it a secret and then told her to keep it quiet. I can't be with someone who lies and doesn't respect my privacy. I haven't spoken to him since Saturday."

"That's what she meant." Carter mumbles, digging his phone out of his pocket.

"What are you talking about?"

He takes a few seconds to pull up something on his phone. "Mom texted me on Saturday after we left. It says 'If Isaac talks to you about anything important, tell him it didn't happen the way he thinks it did. I figured it out on my own and was asked not to say anything.' I asked her what she was talking about, but the only response I got was 'you'll know.' This must be it."

"Call her," I practically growl at Carter. He taps the call button and hands the phone to me. I glance around to make sure we are still the only ones in the room then hit the speaker button.

"Hi, Carter," she answers on the first ring.

"Hey, Mom. I've got you on speaker phone and I'm with Tyson and Isaac."

"Hi, boys."

"Hope, tell me how you found out about Evan and me."

"Oh, well, let's see. We were in the office a couple of weeks ago and I made a comment about the two of you. He didn't do or say anything to indicate you are together, but I see the way you are around each other and I assumed. When I mentioned it, Evan got worried and tried to deny it. I kept pushing and he finally asked me not to say anything to anyone. I agreed. When I saw you two on Saturday, it didn't seem like you were trying to be discreet, so I told you you're a cute couple."

"Shit. I messed up. Badly."

"Have you talked to Evan?" Hope asked.

"Not since Saturday."

"He's a mess. Go talk to him. You clearly love each other and being apart is hurting you both."

"Thanks, Hope."

"Bye, Mom." Carter ends the call. "What are you going to do?"

"Make things right with my boyfriend. I'm sorry about the way I acted this weekend. It won't happen again."

"You can't keep this secret for long. It's going to be better to come out before the media gets ahold of the story. You hold all the cards right now and can come out on your own terms. As obvious as the two of you are, it isn't going to take a genius to figure it out."

"You're right. I need a little more time, but I won't wait long. Now, can you get me back to my car, so I can go see my boyfriend?"

Thirty minutes later, I'm parking in front of Evan's apartment. It's been a crappy few days. I miss Evan so much. Not long after I left his office, before I even made it to the bus, I got one simple text asking me to please talk to him. I ignored it. I'm regretting everything that's happened the past two days, especially hurting Evan.

In the short time we've been together, Evan has learned to trust me and let go of some of the shit Mike put him through. Instead of taking my own advice and trusting the man I love, I treated him like crap and blamed him for something he didn't do. Honestly, I don't deserve his forgiveness, but I hope he gives it to me.

It takes longer than it should for Evan to answer the door and I start to think he isn't going to let me in. I know he's home. His car is parked in his space. I'm about to knock again when it swings open.

When his eyes lock on mine, they are full of hurt and fear. It shatters my heart. I did this to him. After he opened up to me about how much Mike hurt him, I fucking hurt him, too.

"Can we talk?" I ask when Evan doesn't say anything. He remains silent, but steps aside and motions for me to step in.

Reluctantly, I reach for him as he closes the door behind us. Evan steps back, putting a chasm of space between us. It hurts, but I deserve it and more. I run a hand through my short hair. Where do I even begin?

"I'm sorry." It isn't much, but it's a start. Evan continues to stare at me. *Say something.* He doesn't respond to my silent plea, so I dive in. "I'm sorry I hurt you and called you a liar and gossip. I should have listened to you. It may not matter, but I spoke to Hope today and she told me what happened. What you tried to tell me on Saturday. You can thank Carter and Tyson for calling me out on my shit and forcing me to pull my head out of my ass."

"You told them?" he questions.

"Yes. They already suspected. Apparently, I'm not as discreet as I think I am. They said my feelings for you are very obvious when I'm around you."

"I didn't mean to tell your secret."

"You didn't. Hope told me she figured it out on her own, and you tried to deny it. I appreciate you having my back."

"I'll never do anything to betray your trust." Evan's eyes fill with tears as he speaks.

"I know. I was a jerk. I did the one thing I promised not to do. I hurt you and I'm very sorry. I love you so damn much." I take Evan's hand and lead us to the couch, wincing a little when I turn toward him.

"Are you okay? I watched the game. Seeing you lying on the field scared the shit out of me."

"I'm fine. It's a couple of bruised ribs. Nothing that won't heal in a few weeks."

"Can you play?"

"No. I can't practice this week and it's doubtful the doctor will clear me for this week's game. It will probably be closer to two or three weeks before I can get back to it."

"But your family is coming for the game. They won't get to see you play."

"They've seen me play more times than I can count since little league. It's more important that I heal properly. It's my own fault. I was pissed and playing dirty. In a way, I got what I deserved."

"I'm sorry you got hurt, but you were playing like a jerk."

He's right. I took my anger out on the field and if I hadn't gotten hurt, I might have injured someone.

"Are we going to be okay?" I'm not sure I want to hear the answer. Evan might be done with me.

"We're fine. I missed you. I'm glad you came over."

"Me, too. I should have come sooner."

TWENTY-THREE
EVAN

 Nervous does not begin to describe what I feel as I pull up in front of Isaac's house Saturday evening. His family arrived yesterday, and he spent the day with them. Tonight, Isaac invited me over for a cookout and to meet them.

He warned me they are loud and boisterous when they all get together, but I didn't expect to be able to hear them when I got out of the car. Music and loud voices fill the air as I walk to the front door. Before I can knock, the door swings open and I'm greeted by a tall, beautiful woman with dark features, black hair, and the same brown eyes as Isaac.

"You must be Evan!" she gushes.

"Yes."

"I'm Gloria. Isaac's mother."

"It's nice to meet you," I say, offering her my hand.

She ignores my hand and pulls me in for a hug instead. "We hug in this family. It's nice to meet you."

Releasing me, she takes the bag I'm holding and leads me to the kitchen where a man about her age is walking in from the backyard. Beyond him, I see Isaac and a slightly younger version of him on the patio.

"Jose, this is Evan. Evan, this is Isaac's father, Jose."

"It's nice to meet you, young man," Jose says, grabbing me for his own hug. I reluctantly hug him back. This is not like meeting my folks. I doubt there will be any hugging involved. My parents are more formal about greetings. I think I like this way better. I already feel a thousand times more relaxed than when I got out of the car.

Jose goes to the stove and stirs something. Isaac looks like his dad with the exception of having his mom's eyes. Jose is shorter than Isaac, but only by an inch or two. He has brown hair and an olive skin-tone that matches Isaac's. He's very handsome and looks younger than his fifty-three years.

Remembering the bag Gloria took from me, I turn to see that she left it on the counter. I pull out the bottle of bourbon and a set of six glasses I bought at Olde Derby Distillery the last time I visited. I bought eight, so I decided to share the bottle with Isaac's family and give each of them a glass to take home. That will leave Isaac and I with a set of four. I'm not even sure they like bourbon. Maybe this was a bad idea. What was I thinking? I should have asked Isaac before making a decision like this.

I jump when two strong arms wrap around me.

"Hey," Isaac whispers, concern lacing his voice. He turns me toward him and kisses me quickly. I relax a little. "What's wrong?"

"Nothing." I smile and wave him off. The look he gives me tells me he's not buying it. "I brought a bottle of bourbon to share and a glass from my favorite distillery for everyone to take home. I was second guessing myself and now I'm wondering if I made a mistake," I whisper close to his ear so only he can hear me.

"That was a brilliant idea. My family will appreciate the gift."

"Are you sure?"

Isaac leans his head back enough to look me in the eye, but never lets go of my waist. "I'm positive." He kisses me softly and I open my mouth, melting into him as our tongues collide.

A gagging sound and the words "Get a room." From the other side of the kitchen have me pulling away from Isaac as embarrassment heats my face. I can't believe we did that in front of his family.

Isaac flips his brother off and barks, "Bite me, Aiden."

"Nope. That's Evan's job."

Apparently, I wasn't embarrassed enough. I can't imagine how many shades of red I'm turning.

"Enough, Aiden." Jose snaps, but there's humor in his eyes. They are all enjoying this a little too much.

"We're back, Uncle Isaac," a small voice calls as the front door closes, and two precious little girls rush into the kitchen and into Isaac's waiting arms. He hugs them both then looks at me and says, "Evan, these are my nieces, Katie and Kennedy."

"Hi," they say in unison, one much louder than the other. They look so much alike, I hope I can keep them straight.

"Hello, it's nice to meet you both."

The girls wiggle out of Isaac's arms and run off to see their grandmother. A man, who must be Owen, comes into the kitchen carrying a couple of grocery bags.

"Evan, meet my brother, Owen," Isaac introduces. We exchange greetings as Isaac continues. "That little shit over there is Aiden, but you probably figured that out by now.

Aiden waves to Evan and says, "My mom said to tell you I'm sorry if I embarrassed you."

"Boy, don't make me get your father's belt," Gloria snaps, swatting at him.

Aiden jumps out of the way with a laugh. "Dude, I'm twenty-one, you can't smack me."

The look Gloria gives Aiden has me standing at attention. "*I* am not your dude and *you* are never too old to listen to your mother," she scolds.

Aiden actually looks a little timid as he drops his head and mumbles, "Yes, Ma."

Satisfied, Gloria takes the girls' hands and leads them to the backyard. Jose turns off the stove and follows his wife and granddaughters. Isaac puts ice in four of the glasses and starts to pour the bourbon.

"I think it's time for a drink," he declares.

"I definitely need one." Aiden joins us at the counter. "When did you two stop being afraid of Ma?"

"Who says we stopped?" Owen counters and Aiden's eye go wide.

"You're kidding. You have kids, Owen. You can't possibly be scared of that woman."

"That woman is your mother. Show some respect," Isaac reprimands. "Trust us, you will never stop being afraid to cross her."

I laugh at the look of terror on Isaac's face. He must have tried to cross Gloria one too many times.

"Oh, you think this is funny," Aiden teases.

I square my shoulders and look him in the eye. If there's one thing I've learned in the short time I've known the Flores family, it's don't back down. "Extremely. I've never seen three grown men cower at a sweet lady like the three of you."

Aiden takes a step toward me, stopping inches from my face. "I dare you to cross her."

"*I'm* not stupid, college boy," I retort.

Owen and Isaac fall out, laughing their asses off. Aiden holds my gaze for several seconds. I refuse to break eye contact first, so I stand there toe to toe with Isaac's kid brother. Finally, he nods his head a few times.

"Respect." He lifts his fist and I bump it. "I like you." And just like that, I find my place in Isaac's family.

As soon as I start to relax, my brain catches up to what just happened. Oh, shit, I stood up to Aiden. What the hell was I thinking? He could have punched me. Did our exchange make Isaac angry? I don't want him to think I don't like his family. I risk a glance at Isaac then Owen. They're still smiling and giving Aiden crap about being put in his place. I breathe a sigh of relief. Huh, I stood up to someone. So, this is what confidence feels like. It's been a long time since I felt confident or proud. I think I'm finally letting Mike's hold on me fade. Thanks to the safety and trust I feel with Isaac.

An arm wraps around my waist before Isaac kisses my cheek. "I'm proud of you," he whispers. "Watching you handle Aiden was awesome. It's about time someone knocked that cocky ass down a few notches." Isaac's voice is full of humor when he speaks, and I relax even more. This is where I belong. I fit perfectly with Isaac and his family.

Isaac finishes pouring the bourbon and we take our glasses outside and give some to his parents. Isaac and I are drinking ours neat, but the rest of the family has theirs on the rocks. It took a few weeks to convince Isaac that the bourbon doesn't need ice, but now he won't drink it with ice or a mixer. I'll never serve him the crap stuff that needs something added to it to make it drinkable. What's the point?

"Evan, do you want to tell us about this?" Isaac asks, holding up his glass.

"Um, yeah, sure. This is an eighteen-year-old Kentucky straight bourbon with hints of vanilla and caramel. It's from my favorite distillery, Olde Derby Distillery outside of Louisville, Kentucky. I've been there a few times. They produce great bourbons, but this is their best in my opinion. The glasses are their signature glass. They partner with a crystal company out of Oregon and have them specially made. They created the short, curved shape to enhance the flavor. You can each take your glass home."

"Thank you, Evan, this is such a treat," Jose tells me. "I want to make a toast. To having my family together again. And to the first person to make Isaac truly happy. We are glad to finally meet you. Thank you for loving our son. Welcome to the family."

"Don't look so shocked. You're it for me and they know it," Isaac whispers to me. Everyone raises their glasses before taking a drink, while I stand there, mouth open, completely shell shocked. Did that really happen?

TWENTY-FOUR
ISAAC

 Having my family here for a long weekend was great. I was sad to see them leave. They hit it off with Evan and my mom told me that she can see how much we love each other. I wasn't lying when I told Evan he's the one. My mom saw it before I told her my true feelings. We had a great heart to heart on Monday afternoon and she told me that she and Dad really like Evan and they're glad I found someone as amazing as him. They don't know all the details of my relationship with Devante, but they know it didn't end well and I had basically given up on dating or finding the love of my life. I was content with living the bachelor life and convinced myself that I'd be single for the rest of my life.

Since the secret is out to those closest to us, I'm having Tyson and Carter over tonight to hang out with Evan and me. Evan is bringing one of his bourbons to share and some potato salad. I'm cooking burgers and veggie kabobs on the grill. Tyson and Carter will likely show up with something to add to the table.

Evan and I spent a couple of hours in bed this afternoon. I considered taking a shower with him, but that would have probably ended in amazing shower sex and possibly another round between the sheets. We didn't have time for that, so I took a quick shower first then forced myself to the kitchen while Evan got ready. I'd never hear the end of it if our friends showed up and we weren't able to answer the door. It would have totally been worth it, but there was no way I was convincing Evan. He's kind of a rule follower.

Evan joins me in the kitchen, freshly showered, looking like sex on a stick with his damp hair, a pair of tight black jeans and fitted green t-shirt. He's been working out at the gym in his complex and between the days spent there and the times we go to the beach, he has gained some muscle mass and darkened his tan. It a sexy combination that makes me want to lick him constantly. The green shirt was a little loose the first time I saw him in it a couple of months ago. Now, it hugs his tight body. Even though I can't see his six pack, I know what's hiding under the shirt and I want nothing more than to rip it off of him.

He walks up to me and uses his thumb to wipe the side of my mouth. "You're drooling," he teases, pulling me out of my lustful thoughts.

"What?" I ask, running the back of my hand over my mouth. "No, I wasn't."

Evan doubles over with laughter. "You weren't, but you were staring pretty damn hard."

"Something's hard alright," I mumble.

"How? How can you possibly be hard? We just went one round on the couch and two in the bed."

"What can I say? I can't get enough of you."

"Me either, but I'm spent."

"Eh, maybe it's your age," I tease.

"You better take that back," he growls.

"You are pushing thirty."

"I have over two years."

"You'll be twenty-eight in less than a month. You can call it two years."

"You aren't that much younger than me."

"I won't be twenty-five until January. I'm more than three years younger. Apparently, it makes a difference."

"It's a good thing I like our friends or I might be inclined to go home and leave you with nothing but your hand to handle your needs."

I gasp in horror. "You wouldn't."

"Are you sure about that?"

Before he has a chance to realize what's happening, I grab Evan and pull him into my arms, kissing him deeply. Our tongues collide and the feel of him against me sends a shudder through me. My dick hardens and I'm a little surprised. Teasing Evan is fun, but honestly, I'm not sure I have another round in me right now.

"Ah, Jesus, do you two ever keep your hands off each other?" Tyson bellows.

Evan jumps back at the sound of Tyson's voice. I knew I should have kept the door locked. I thought it was a smart idea in case we were outside at the grill, but now I'm regretting that decision, especially since it embarrassed Evan.

"Fuck off," I bark in return, causing Tyson and Carter to double over laughing.

Evan busies himself pulling toppings out of the refrigerator. I glare at my friends, but they're totally unfazed by the fact they embarrassed my boyfriend. I'm mad they upset Evan but amused by the situation.

Tyson and Carter place a tray of chicken wings and

several bags of chips and dip on the counter while I walk over to Evan and take a few items from him.

"You okay?"

He nods, but won't look at me. Shit. I hate that he gets embarrassed and upset so easily. I know it's because of the things that asshole ex of his did to him.

"They were just teasing. They love you," I whisper even though Tyson and Carter have retreated to the other side of the room to give us some privacy.

"I know. I'm sorry. Why am I such a mess?"

"You're not a mess," I say, turning him toward me. "It's okay to kiss me in front of our friends. We didn't do anything wrong."

He nods slightly. "I'm okay. Let's enjoy the night." Evan smiles at me then continues placing condiments on the counter and pulling out the plate of onions, lettuce, and tomato we cut this morning.

Rather than making any more of a fuss, I accept that Evan is fine and go on about our night. It isn't fair to him to make a big deal out of his reaction in front of our friends, but it bothers me that something as small as getting caught kissing sends him into a spiral. I need to let it go. This is all new for both for us. I'm a little surprised at myself for being so bold and open in front of Tyson and Carter. Maybe it's because I know them well and trust them. I've forced Evan to keep us a secret and then got angry at him when I thought he betrayed me. Now, I'm only willing to let a few select people know about us. It has to make him feel unsure about our relationship and my love for him especially after everything Mike put him through.

"Tyson," I call, gaining his attention. "The grill should be hot by now. Can you and Carter go put the burgers and kabobs on?" I ask, handing him two trays of food. I try to silently communicate that I need a minute with my boyfriend.

He must understand because he takes the trays with a nod. "You got it. Carter, grab some tongs."

When Carter closes the door behind them, I turn to Evan, take his hand and lead him to our, eh, my bedroom. Where did that thought come from? I'm not sure, but I like the idea of sharing a home with Evan.

When we reach the bedroom, I face my boyfriend and cup his cheek. "Hey, I'm sorry if them seeing us like that embarrassed you, but I want you to know, I'm all in. I'm not ready for the world to know, but I won't hide in front of my family, our friends, or Hope. Just so you know, I regret not meeting your parents and I think next time you talk to them; you should share the news."

"What? Are you sure? Isaac, I'm sorry I told Hope and the guys found out. I feel really bad about it, and I don't want you to feel like my parents have to know."

"Stop. I meant every word I said. I want your parents to know, and I want you to be comfortable around Tyson and Carter."

A smile tugs at his lips as he relaxes into my touch. "Thank you."

"One more thing. No more apologizing for people finding out. You did not do anything wrong, and I never should have blamed you. It's in our past and we've both apologized. There's no reason to keep reliving it."

"Really?"

"Absolutely."

"I love you so much." Evan kisses me quickly. "It's time to have some fun with our friends."

Our friends. I like the sound of that and I'm grateful Tyson, Carter, and Evan hit it off and get along. I want Evan to be part of everything in my world, but for that to truly happen, I have to quit hiding who I am.

TWENTY-FIVE
EVAN

Isaac's ribs are much better and at his appointment this morning, the doctor told him he can start light workouts today. If those go well, he will be able to return to practice in a few days and play in next Sunday's game. The relief in Isaac's voice when he called me with the news was a welcome sound. Being off the field has been weighing heavy on him these past weeks. He feels like he's letting his team down, especially because the injury could have been avoided if he hadn't let his anger get the best of him.

I've been trying to come up with a way to celebrate the good news from the doctor and do something fun and different for our date tonight. We've fallen into this routine of taking turns planning what to do each night. Most of the time, one of us cooks and we stay in because we're tired from the day. I decided I like the idea of staying home tonight but wanted to do more than simply cook and watch TV.

When I hear Isaac's key in the door, I scramble up off the floor to greet him. A couple of weeks ago we exchanged keys.

It was a big step and one I don't take lightly. I've never given anyone a key to my place before for two reasons. One, my place was my parents' place and two, I've never trusted anyone the way I trust Isaac.

I can't hide the huge grin on my face when Isaac opens the door. He takes three steps into the apartment and freezes, eyes going wide with wonder and excitement as he takes in the living room that's been transformed into one hell of a blanket fort. I'm damn proud of my work.

"It's our date."

"What exactly are we doing on this date?"

"Well." I take his hand, leading him to the fort entrance. "This is a blanket fort. It's a special place built only for the one I love most. No one else has ever been inside one of my famous blanket forts. Unless you count my parents, who joined me a few times when I was a little kid." Isaac stares as me unblinking as I continue. "Blanket forts are magical places where anything you dream can happen." I drop to my knees and crawl inside, motioning for Isaac to follow. He crawls in behind and looks all around in complete disbelief.

"You did all of this today? It must have taken hours."

Blankets cover almost the entire room, giving us plenty of space to stretch out and relax. On the side that borders the wall, I have pillows lined up. White Christmas lights are strung across the top of the fort and down the sides, giving us some soft, romantic light. A large blanket is laid out on the floor with a picnic basket and bottle of wine.

"Sit," I command, pointing to the pillows. While Isaac gets comfortable, I open the bottle of red wine and pour each of us a glass. After handing one to Isaac, I prop myself up next to him and hand him several small strips of paper and a pen. "So, here's what I'm thinking. While we sip on our wine, we each choose ten questions we want to ask the other person and write each one on a strip of paper. Then we fold them up and put them in this bowl. While we have our picnic dinner, we play a slightly altered version of Twenty Questions. We will take turns drawing a question and reading it out loud then we both have to answer."

"What kind of questions?"

"Anything you want to ask. It can be simple like 'What is your favorite color?' or it can be dirty," I add with a wink.

"Okay, we each write ten?" he questions.

"Yes." Isaac takes the paper and pen and immediately writes three questions. What the hell? I've known all day I was planning this date and I haven't come up with one single question. I need to get to work.

We spend the next fifteen minutes or so writing down our questions in silence. Concentrating is difficult with Isaac steadily writing. How is he so good at this? When we both have the questions written and folded, I pile two plates with egg salad and pimento cheese sandwiches, chips, pickles and olives, and a scoop of fruit salad. After handing a plate to Isaac, I refill our wine glasses and move back to sit next to him.

"Are you ready to play?" I ask a little unsure about this idea of mine.

"Fuck, yeah, I'm ready."

Great, his excitement has me even more concerned about the kind of questions he wrote down.

"You draw first." I hand Isaac the bowl. He pulls a strip out and opens it, laughing when he reads the paper.

"I guess we're starting a little intense." He takes a deep breath and lets it out slowly. I wonder who wrote the question and what it can possibly be. I don't think any of mine were intense, funny, maybe, but not intense. My heart races with anticipation. "Do you want kids and if so, how many?"

Shit. He definitely wrote that question and it is... intense. This is something I know the answer to, but I'm not sure I'm ready to have this talk. It was my idea, so there is no way I'm getting out of this.

"Yes. I want kids. I'm not sure how many, but I'm thinking two or three at least."

Isaac stares at me for a beat them beams. "Really! You want kids?"

"Yeah. Do you?"

"Absolutely. I've always imagined having a big family but never thought I would meet someone who wanted them, too."

"How many kids are in 'a big family'?"

"Five or six." I choke on my wine at his answer.

"You want five or six kids?"

"Yep. And I want to adopt them. There are so many kids who need good homes. They deserve to have a family who loves them. No surrogates for me."

I didn't know it was possible to love this man more, but listening to him talk about adopting kids is causing all kinds of feelings to stir. I'm not sure about six kids, but I can see us having four.

"Wow, that's a great idea. I always knew I wanted to have kids. I never thought about how I would have those kids. You're right, there are a lot of kids who need a family. I would be open to adopting."

"I think we just implied that *we* should adopt children together." Isaac looks at me with so much love then leans over and give me a chaste kiss. "I would love nothing more than having a family with you."

I can't breathe for a second. Isaac Flores wants to have children with me. This might be the best date idea in the history of date ideas and we're only on question one.

"Your turn." Isaac shakes the bowl in front of me, pulling me out of my daydream.

I grab a strip of paper, reading the question silently. These papers need to be shuffled. This is another Isaac question. Trying not to be embarrassed, I read it out loud. "How old were you when you lost your virginity?"

He stares at me for long seconds. The longer he takes to answer the question, the more I worry about the answer. Was he that young? Finally, he drops his head and whispers, "Twenty."

Shock. Complete shock is all I feel. There's nothing wrong with being twenty when you lose your virginity, but I was positive Isaac would have lost it a lot younger. I mean look at him.

"I didn't see that coming," I joke.

He smirks at me. "And how old were you?"

"I don't think you want to know the answer."

"Oh, no, it doesn't matter if you were older. You have to play. Spill."

I look him in the eye, confidence coursing through me and say in my sassiest voice, "Fifteen. I've got five whole years on you, smart ass."

"Oh, you think you're so much better than me. Let's skip to another one of my questions," he playfully snaps, tossing the bowl on the floor. "How many sexual partners have you had?"

"You don't play by the rules."

"Rules be damned. Answer the question," he growls.

"Five."

Hmmm, five in twelve years. Not bad. Not as impressive as my ten in four years, but not everyone can be me."

"Cocky bastard," I whisper.

Isaac tackles me, hovering over my body, causing all sorts

of fireworks to ping through my body. He leans down, crashing his lips onto mine and pushing his tongue into my mouth. My arms wrap around him, pulling him closer so I can feel his erection against my leg. He breaks the kiss and pushes himself off of me and sits back against the pillows.

"Let's see what else we can learn. This is fun," he states calmly as if I'm not completely worked up. How can he go from a passionate kiss to acting like we're two buddies hanging out? "My turn." He picks up the bowl and grabs another strip. "Ooh, this one's good. If you had to completely change careers, what would your new job be?"

"Teacher."

"What? Really?"

"Yeah. When I was a kid, I loved going to school and helping the teacher. For a while I thought about becoming a teacher then decided not to go to college. When I was offered my first promotion at the stadium, I realized I actually liked working there, so I changed my mind about college and got a degree in hospitality management."

"Cool. I think you'd make a great teacher."

"What about you?"

"I've never given it much thought. If I hadn't gotten drafted out of high school, I would have gone to college, but I have no idea what I would have majored in. I am interested in how the body heals and any time I've been injured and had to go to PT, I've always asked a lot of in-depth questions. Physical therapist might be a cool job if I wasn't playing ball."

"If we ever need new career, we have a starting point."

"That we do." Isaac hands me the bowl and I draw again.

Yes! I definitely want to know the answer to this one. It's something I've wanted to bring up for weeks, but never got the courage, so I wrote it down tonight. "Have you ever played with a sex toy?" Isaac chokes on his wine when I read the question. Interesting. The words 'sex toy' get him flustered.

He clears his throat, "Um, actually, no, not unless my hand counts."

"It doesn't. Why not?"

"That's a whole new question."

"I don't care. Answer it."

"I've thought about it, but it felt weird to play with one alone even though that's sort of the point of a toy. You're only my second boyfriend and it isn't something that's ever come up before. I'm not opposed to them."

"Good," I exclaim with a satisfied smile.

"Wait. Have you played with them? Are you saying you want us to play with them?" Isaac's face is a mix of interest and fear. I get it. I wasn't sure the first time I tried to use a toy, but when Mike lost interest in the sex part of our relationship, I decided to take care of myself.

"Yes, and yes. They're fun alone, so I can only imagine how much fun they'll be together."

Isaac lets out a frustrated growl and, not so discreetly, adjusts himself. "You're killing me," he groans. "We can't keep talking about sex."

"Why not?" I ask in the most innocent voice I can muster.

"Because if we do, I'm going to take you right here."

"We're definitely having fort sex, but not until after we answer all the questions," I tell him shaking the bowl of paper in his face.

Isaac grabs it from me and opens a question, "What is one place you've always wanted to visit? Ireland," he answers quickly as he pulls the next one.

"When do you feel most loved by me? Always."

He reads another one, "Do you need anything more from

me in our relationship? No. You're everything I've ever wanted in a man."

He unfolds another slip, "What do you find sexy about me. Everything." He tosses the bowl aside. "I can't wait any longer."

Then he's on top of me and clothes are flying.

TWENTY-SIX
ISAAC

 It's been three weeks since my injury and I missed two games. Getting back to practice today was great. I was starting to go a little insane with boredom. I'm looking forward to a quiet evening with Evan. Instead of taking a shower at the stadium, I rushed home to meet him. I didn't want to wait any longer to see my man. When I emerge from the bathroom, he's sitting at my kitchen table with his laptop and a glass of red wine. I pour myself a glass and join him, leaning for a quick kiss.

"What's this?"

"My reviews. I've been trying to get up the nerve to look at them for a month. Hope told me the ones she saw were good, but I was still afraid to look at them."

"Was she right? I can't imagine anyone giving you a bad review," I tell him, thinking more about the mind-blowing fort sex we had a few nights ago than his job. We also spent time the next day ordering a few sex toys online. I can't wait to try them out.

"You would be wrong there." Evan's voice pulls me from my sexy memory. I focus on him and listen intently. "I do have three bad reviews, but they are from the same employee, and he is basically a pissed-off jerk who thought he could intimidate me and get paid without doing any actual work. His reviews were written the two times I wrote him up and then the day I fired him. I really don't care what he thinks."

"What about the others?"

"They are all great. My lowest rating is a 4 and most of them are 5s. Hope told me this, but I didn't believe her. The comments are really nice 'Best boss ever.' 'Evan is easy to work for and treats us fairly.' 'Evan doesn't mind stepping in and working alongside his employees any time there is a need for extra hands.' I can't believe they like me."

"I have no doubt they love you. You are great at your job."

"Enough of this," he says, closing the computer. "I want to spend time with you. How was your first day back at practice?"

"Rough. I'm exhausted. Doing practically nothing for two weeks makes it difficult to get back into the action. I'm sore as hell, but the hot shower helped."

"I wouldn't say you did *nothing*. You certainly did *something* last night and a few nights ago," he reminds me. Memories of last night flash in my mind. It was fun, but not as much fun as the sex we had in the blanket fort a few nights ago. Those are damn good images.

"More like *someone*," I growl.

"I'll rub your sore muscles tonight after dinner." He pats my leg and starts to stand up, but I pull him back to the chair kissing him again.

I break the kiss and growl, "Oh, I have a muscle you can rub." I put Evan's hand on my hardening cock.

Evan rubs one hand over my shorts, while the other

snakes its way up my chest and around my neck, pulling me in for another kiss. My phone rings, but I ignore it and deepen the kiss. Pushing his chair back, Evan drops to his knees and pulls on my shorts. I lift myself enough for him to get the shorts from under me and he pulls them down to my ankles. My phone rings again, but I'm focused on Evan licking my thighs and ignore the call. People need to leave me the hell alone. I'm a little busy.

"Oh, god," I moan as Evan licks up my shaft then takes me in his mouth.

I wrap a hand in his hair and push him down further. He chokes a little, so I release him. He lifts his mouth to my tip before sliding it down my shaft again. Shit, that feels good.

He bobs his head up and down slowly at first then faster for a few minutes before slowing down again. It's driving me fucking mad. Every time I get close, he slows down, torturing me in the best possible way.

I've ignored two more calls, reveling in the feel of Evan's mouth on me. He slides his mouth down slowly until I hit the back of his throat. He cups my balls with one hand and gently squeezes them while pinching my nipple with the other hand, and I explode into his throat. Shit, that didn't last long enough.

He sits back in his chair, licking his lips with a satisfied smile.

"Proud of yourself?"

"Yep."

"Thank you." I kiss him. "That was amazing. It's my turn to take care of you." As I stand up, planning to carry him to the bedroom, my phone rings again. I let out a deep sigh.

"You need to see who it is." He's right. My phone never rings this many times in a row. It stops as I reach for it. To my horror, I find six missed calls from my dad and several texts from my family.

> Dad: Call me, son.
>
> Owen: You need to call me or Dad.
>
> Owen: Answer your damn phone.

"Shit. Something's wrong. Look." I show the texts to Evan. He takes my hand and holds onto it while I call my dad, putting it on speaker. If this is serious, I need Evan to hear. My heart sinks, imagining all the things that could possibly be wrong. It has to be my mom since Dad and Owen are the ones calling. The thought of something happening to my mom horrifies me. She's the glue that holds our family together. She's the best mom and wife and we'd all be lost without her. Dad picks up after several rings.

"Isaac," Dad says. "Hey, Son."

"Dad what's going on?"

He takes a deep breath and my heart sinks.

"It's Aiden. He was in a car accident," Dad drops an unexpected bomb on me.

"What? When? Where? Is he okay?" I word vomit, not sure what to ask. I'm relieved mom is okay, but knowing something bad happened to my little brother is whole other level of terror.

"We don't know much. He was driving back to his apartment after class. Someone t-boned him on the driver's side. We got to the hospital a few minutes ago and are waiting to see the doctor and talk to the police."

My heart is racing and my entire body is shaking. My baby brother is hurt and there's not a damn thing I can do. Evan squeezes my hand, but it barely registers.

"Thank you, Mr. Flores. Call us when you know more."

"Take care of my boy."

"I've got him." Evan ends the call and looks at me.

"Why did you hang up?" I yell, grabbing my phone. Evan gently takes it out of my hand and places it on the other side of the table, then he takes my other hand, holding both of mine and turning me to face him fully.

"Where did you go?" he asks.

"What do you mean?"

"I mean you stopped talking in the middle of the conversation."

"Oh, I guess I was thinking about Aiden. Did I miss something?"

"The doctor came in. They are going to call us back after they talk to him."

I pull away from Evan and pace the kitchen for several minutes. Why didn't I answer the phone? My family needed me, and I ignored them for a stupid blow job.

"Stop beating yourself up."

"I'm not!" I bark

"Not stopping or not beating yourself up?"

"Neither. Both. I don't know!" I cry. I place both hands on the counter and drop my head. My chest tightens, my body shakes, and my vision blurs. How can this be happening? My little brother is lying in a damn hospital bed and there's nothing I can do. I can't go to him. I can't help him. I'm useless.

Evan walks over to me and pulls me in for a hug. I melt into him, feeling safe and comforted in his arms. He leads me to the couch and gently pushes me to sit before he walks away and comes back a few seconds later with my phone and two glasses of wine.

"There is nothing we can do but wait. Try not to worry

until we know more. I know that's an impossible request, but let's try."

I take the glass and nod as he sits next to me, taking my hand in his again. It's a simple gesture, but it means more than he'll ever know. Without Evan by my side, I'd probably be driving to the airport right now.

By the time the phone rings again, I am on my third glass of wine and made it damn clear I need something stronger, but Evan refuses to give me bourbon. At this point, I'd like to down half a bottle of Tequila and forget everything.

"Dad, how is he?" I don't bother with formal greetings.

I hate feeling this way–scared, lost, devastated, shattered. Is there a strong enough word to describe the range of emotions I've felt over the past hour?

"Stable. I'm sorry it took so long, but we talked to the doctor and the police. The guy who hit him was drunk. Drunk at four in the afternoon. Can you believe it? Aiden is lucky that the back door took the brunt of the impact. We would be having a very different conversation if the driver's door would have taken a direct hit," Jose chokes on his last sentence, pausing briefly to get his emotions in check before continuing. "He has a broken leg, broken arm, collapsed lung, and a few broken ribs. Nothing life threatening, but he'll need surgery on his leg. Basically, the entire left side of his body is broken."

"That doesn't sound good."

"He'll heal, Isaac. It will take time and when he wakes up, he probably won't be happy about having to leave school and move home, but we think that is the best thing for him. He won't be able to drive for a while. If he's at home, your mother and I can take him to all his doctors' appointments and PT when the time comes."

I breathe a sigh of relief. My dad is right. Aiden is alive

and all his injuries will heal. In a few months, he'll be back to his normal life. I need to be thankful.

"How is Mom?"

"She's better now that we have some good news. But you know your mom. She can't stand to see any of you hurt. It took seeing you in person to convince her that your ribs were only bruised. Even though visiting hours are over and he's an adult, she refuses to leave his room. The nurses gave up arguing with her and brought a cot for her to sleep on tonight. I'm in the waiting room right now, but I think I'm going to get a hotel room for a few days, so we will have somewhere to shower and relax. Owen left the girls with a neighbor. Now that we know Aiden is going to be okay, he's going to make the three-hour drive home after we grab some dinner."

"Please call me tomorrow with an update or sooner if anything changes."

"I will, Isaac. Get some sleep and let Evan take care of you. I know you're worried but try to focus on football. You have a big game on Sunday."

"I will," I agree. Leave it to my dad to keep me in line from more than a thousand miles away. "I love you. Tell Mom, Owen, and Aiden I love them."

"I love you, Son. I will pass it on to the family."

I end the call and fall into Evan's arms, crying until I have nothing left inside. I have no idea why it took getting good news before I sobbed, but now I can't stop. Evan holds me, stroking my hair for a few minutes then rubbing a hand up and down my back.

"I'm glad he's going to be okay," Evan whispers.

"Me, too. Thank you for being here with me."

"I'll always be here for you. I'm going to get us some dinner. You rest."

"Please let me help. I need to do something, or my mind is going to go to all sorts of negative places."

Evan stands up and holds a hand out to me. He leads me to the kitchen, and we quietly prepare dinner together. It's romantic, domestic, and intimate. It's home, safety, and comfort. It's everything I've ever wanted but didn't know I needed.

TWENTY-SEVEN
EVAN

 The front door opens and a few seconds later, Isaac pulls me into his arms. It comforts me knowing he has a key, so he can come and go as he pleases. He did the same for me. It was a big step for us, but one I'm glad we took. It's one more brick out of my wall and one more leap away from Mike's hold. I turn to face Isaac and give him a quick kiss before turning back to the pot on the stove.

"What are you making?" he asks, looking over my shoulder.

"Chicken noodle soup. Early November is the perfect time of year for the first pot of soup back home. I was feeling nostalgic, so I made some."

"Sounds and smells delicious."

"How's Aiden?" his accident was almost a week ago and we've been getting daily updates. Poor Isaac is still worried. He's like his mom in that respect. I don't think he'll be completely convinced until he sees Aiden.

"A little better. I talked to him this morning. The surgery

went well yesterday. He's in a good bit of pain today, but they are managing it. Dad said if there are no complications, he will go home in three or four days. They are going to have to rent a van to get him home. The car is too small for him to stretch out in for the three-hour drive."

"I'm glad to hear he's improving."

"Me, too." Isaac gets a bottle of water from the refrigerator and walks over to the kitchen table to relax while I tend to the soup.

"Evan?" Isaac questions, concern lacing my name. "What is this?"

I glance over to where he's standing. Embarrassment heats my face when I realize what I left on the kitchen table in full view. Then anger hits me and I drop the wooden spoon. It hits the edge of the counter then falls to the floor, splattering soup all over the front of the cabinet.

"Why the fuck are you invading my privacy?" I snap, grabbing the paper from his hands. "This is none of your business."

"You're the one who left it on the table," he argues.

"That doesn't give you the right to look at it."

"It wasn't on purpose. That enormous number wasn't easy to ignore."

"Well, fucking ignore it," I bark as I fold the credit card bill and shove it in my pocket. Then I return to the stove. Ignoring the mess I made, I take another spoon out of the drawer and pretend the soup needs my undivided attention.

After several minutes, Isaac comes up behind me and wraps his arms around me. "Put the spoon down," he whispers calmly. I pause for several seconds while he waits, never letting go of me. Slowly, I place the spoon on the rest. Isaac gently guides me away from the stove before turning me to face him.

"I'm sorry. You're right, I shouldn't have looked at your bill. I can't change what happened or forget what I saw. Talk to me. Are you in trouble?"

"You just saw a credit card bill for over fifty thousand dollars. What do you think?"

"Is that the only one?"

I swallow hard before answering. "No," I state simply. Isaac stares at me, waiting for me to say more. I sigh heavily "It's the highest, but I have three others all around twenty thousand. Plus, my car payment. It's the only reason I rent my apartment. I couldn't get approved for a loan to purchase a house."

"Jesus, Evan, that's more than a hundred thousand in debt. How did that happen?"

"Well, excuse the fuck out of me for not making five *million* dollars a year catching a damn ball."

"Fifteen," he mumbles.

"What?"

"Never mind."

"Wait. Are you saying you make fifteen million dollars a year?"

"That's not important."

I scoff as I push away from Isaac. "You need to go."

"Fuck, no! We need to talk about this."

"No, we don't. I'm drowning under my debt and you're banking millions. We are not the same."

"Please let me help you."

"Absolutely not. I'm not taking money from you."

"Good because I'm not offering to pay your debt. I *am* offering to help you budget and crawl out of the hole you dug."

"What do you know about budgeting?"

"I grew up very poor and had to think about every penny I

spent. I worked in high school and gave most of that money to my parents to help pay bills. My first two years in the NFL, I lived in the cheapest place I could find and saved every penny possible until I had enough saved to help my parents and brothers. I pay for Aiden to go to college, and I bought my parents a home, so they could stop renting. I still save a bunch of money every year and share it with my family. When I bought my home, I found something modest. The only reason I chose a gated community is for safety. I don't need crazy fans or paparazzi following me and invading my personal life. I know how to budget. I can help you."

"No, you can't. I've been accumulating debt for years. Every time I try to pay shit off, I end up doing great for a couple of months then I find something I can't live without, and I buy it."

"What are you buying?" he asks, looking around my minimalist apartment. I have very little furniture, dishes, or décor."

I drop my head unable to look him in the eyes. He's never going to understand. This is where our relationship will likely end. He'll get to see the real me, things I keep hidden from everyone. Isaac reaches over, placing a finger under my chin and slowly lifting my face to his. Then he presses a gentle kiss on my lips before taking my hand and leading me to the couch.

"Please talk to me. I can see the hurt and fear in your eyes. I'm not going to judge you. I love you, Evan, and I want to help you."

After several minutes, I finally whisper, "Bourbon." It's one simple word. Admission of a problem I've been hiding for the past six years.

"What?" He stares at me in complete shock, opening and closing his mouth several times. "Do you have a drinking problem? I've only seen you drunk twice and it was because we had a few too many glasses of wine."

"I don't have a drinking problem. I have a purchasing problem. I've taken trips to almost every bourbon distillery in the country. I purchase high-end bourbons and have shelves and shelves of the stuff in my closet. I enjoy it, but I buy it a lot faster than I drink it. Between the trips and the bottles, I've managed to run up quite the credit card debt."

"How much do you spend on these bottles of bourbon? I've seen some at the store for hundreds of dollars."

A humorless laugh escapes me, "No, hundreds is for the minor leagues. I play with the big boys. I have bottles that cost as much as eight and ten thousand dollars."

Isaac chokes at my admission, "Ten thousand dollars for a bottle of liquor?"

"The one I'm dying to get my hands on is a bottle of 40-year-old Kentucky straight bourbon that sells for eighteen thousand. There are only about a hundred bottles in existence."

Isaac stares at me wide-eyed. I get it. It's hard for most people to understand spending that kind of money on alcohol.

"Evan," he finally starts. "You can't keep doing this."

"Don't you think I know that? I can't help it. I've tried. I have zero self-control."

"That's not true. You have plenty of restraint when it comes to other things in your life. Why is this different?" he asks.

"I'm not sure."

"Okay, well, let's try to make a plan for how to get the debt paid off. Do you have any savings?"

"A little. Every month I'm torn between paying extra on my credit card bills or adding some to savings. Most months, by the time I pay the minimums and my other bills, there isn't much left."

"Can I see your bills and help you make a plan?"

"I guess." I want Isaac to help me because I will never be able to do it on my own, but I don't want him to see how bad things are for me. Reluctantly, I go to my bedroom to get my computer and the stack of bills sitting next to it. I set everything up at the kitchen table and step back so Isaac can look through it all. While he peruses my bills, periodically asking questions, I busy myself finishing dinner preparation. I mix up a box of cornbread and put it in the oven while the soup simmers.

"Come sit," he instructs after over an hour.

After pulling the cornbread from the oven, I drop into the chair next to him, terrified to hear what he's going to say.

"You make good money and if you follow my plan, we can get you out of this debt in no time."

I don't believe Isaac, but instead of telling him that, I respond, "Okay, let's hear it."

"You have fifteen thousand in your savings account. Close the account and use it to pay off this credit card," he says handing me the lowest one that's just over seventeen thousand. "I know depleting your savings can be scary, but I think in the long run, it will be for the best. It's not earning you any interest, so I don't see the point. You have your 401k investments, and your car is relatively new. There shouldn't be any major expenses coming your way anytime soon and if you have any health-related stuff come up, you have insurance."

"Okay, but my saving won't pay that bill completely."

"No, but you have other expenses you can cut. Do you need eight different streaming services and two music services?"

"Not really." I shrug. "I only use one of my music apps

and I tend to use two or three of the streaming services more than the others."

We work through each bill over the next hour. By the time we finish, I have cut my monthly expenses down by over a thousand dollars. I had no idea I was wasting so much money each month on crap I rarely use. Cutting out those expenses and closing my savings account will leave me with enough money to pay off the entire debt on the lowest card during the next billing cycle. If I follow Isaac's budget, use coupons when I go to the grocery store, and stop using my credit cards, my debt will be paid off in about a year. Maybe a little longer. Then I can start banking money each month and save for those expensive bottles that I want. The more I think about it, the bourbon might mean a little more to me if I work for it rather than taking the easy way and charging it. What felt like the easy way for so many years, got me in massive amounts of debt that does nothing but stress me out. Relief washes over me. I feel like a huge weight has been lifted off my shoulders. I'm a little overwhelmed and shocked that this is doable. I can't believe I can afford to pay off my debt so quickly.

"Thank you," I tell Isaac before leaning in for a kiss.

"You're welcome. Let's eat. I'm starving."

The chicken noodle soup is going to be delicious. It's even better when it has time to simmer. Isaac is going to love this recipe. I ladle soup into two bowls and hand one to Isaac. It fills my heart to feed my man.

TWENTY-EIGHT
ISAAC

 When I leave Evan's apartment early the next morning, I'm still reeling from this new knowledge about him. We all have our vices. Look at me, I can't get enough fast-food or boy bands, and I'm forcing Evan to keep us a secret, but thousands upon thousands of dollars in debt for brown liquid is insane. If he hadn't shown me the shelves of unopened bourbon in his closet, I would have worried that he has a drinking problem, too. Although, as much time as we spend together, I know he never gets completely wasted and there have only been a few nights he's had more than a couple glasses. Still, part of me questions if that's why he's dating me. I hate that thought. I don't want to wonder if Evan is with me for my money. I know better, but that doesn't keep my mind from going where it shouldn't.

This morning, I pretended to be asleep when he left for work. As soon as he was out the door, I bolted. I've been driving aimlessly for the past forty-five minutes, too worked up to go home. It's not like I'll be able to relax. I've got to get my head on straight before practice.

My experience with Devante wasn't much different than Evan's experience with Mike. They both used us in some way. I chose not to share much with Evan for a couple of reasons. One, it's been three years and I thought I had moved on, and two, Devante used me for my money unlike Mike who used Evan as a metaphorical punching bag. Devante expected me to pay for everything–dates, his bills, anything he needed. I was young and dumb and fell right into his trap. He even convinced me to buy him a car and get a credit card in his name.

When we broke up, I let him keep the car and all the stuff I bought him. I closed the credit card but didn't ask him to pay me back for anything. It wasn't worth it. I cared more about keeping my sexuality a secret than I cared about the money. It pains me to admit, I paid him hush money, too. I gave him five hundred thousand dollars to keep his mouth shut about our relationship. No one knows that. Tyson knows about everything else, but not the hush money. I keep that to myself. It's an embarrassing admission that isn't anyone's business.

It's barely eight in the morning when I find myself parking in front of Tyson's condo. I shoot off a quick text telling him I'm here, so he will buzz me in then I take the elevator up to the top floor. He has a modern penthouse condo on the top floor of a seventy-five-story building overlooking Miami Beach with breathtaking views. When I step off the private elevator and into the hallway outside the penthouse, he is waiting for me in the open doorway.

"You look like hell."

"Thanks."

"Come on in."

I follow him into the spacious room with floor-to-ceiling windows and panoramic views. It's a huge open space. Down one hallway is the master suite, a small living room, and a home theater. Down the other are five bedrooms, and five bathrooms, one for his sister, Grace, and one for each of her four children. After her husband died in a small plane crash several years ago, Tyson bought this place, so she'd have a somewhere to live when she relocated to Miami to be close to family. His parents and her in-laws have their own apartments in the same building.

"Where are Grace and the kids?" I ask, walking into the quiet space.

"Grace took the kids to school. She'll be back soon. Coffee?"

"Yeah, thanks."

He pours us each a cup and gestures for me to sit on the couch. I sink on the soft, leather surface and take a long drink of the hot coffee. I'm not sure why I'm here. Hell, I didn't even register the drive here.

"Something on your mind?" he asks when I'm quiet for too long.

"Too damn much," I reply with a shake of my head.

"Did something happen between you and Evan?"

"Sort of."

"You aren't making this easy, Isaac," he growls.

"I'm trying to figure out what to tell you. I don't want to say something that's going to embarrass or hurt Evan."

"That tells me quite a bit."

"What exactly does that tell you?" I snap.

"That whatever happened might be eating away at you, but you still love him and it didn't damage your relationship."

"We didn't break up or really even have a fight. He has some money problems. We spent hours last night working up a plan and budget. If he follows it, everything will be fine, and he can fix the issue."

"I'm not seeing the problem."

"I tossed and turned all night. All I can think about is this is a repeat of all the shit I went through with Devante."

"Did Evan ask you for money?"

"No."

"Did you offer him money?"

"No."

"Did anything that happened last night or at any time in your relationship give you the impression that Evan wants money from you?"

"No."

"So, what you're telling me is Evan is nothing like Devante."

I don't bother responding. He's right. Evan is nothing like Devante. He pays his own way and the first thing he said last night was he will not take money from me. Instead of trusting his word, I let my past get the best of me and refused to trust him. Looks like Evan isn't the only one with trust issues.

"Thanks for the coffee." I leave my mug on the counter and rush toward the door.

"What are you going to do?"

"Go talk to Evan. He needs to know the truth about my past. He trusted me with his secret. I have to trust him with mine."

"See you at practice," Tyson says following me to the door. "Don't let hot office sex make you late."

I step onto the elevator and flip him off right before the door closes.

Less than an hour later, I'm standing in the hallway outside of Evan and Hope's offices, wiping my sweaty palms on my shorts and trying to calm the anxiety that's been building the entire drive here. Admitting what I allowed Devante to do is like admitting weakness and I never want Evan to think I'm weak. One last deep breath before I walk into the office. Hope is sitting at her desk and I can see Evan in his office, typing away on his computer.

"Good morning. You can go in," she tells me.

Slowly, I walk the short distance to the doorway and knock on the jamb. Evan looks up from his computer and smiles.

"Good morning," he greets, standing up and walking to me. When he gets close, his demeanor changes. "Are you okay?"

"Do you have a few minutes to talk?" His face falls as he nods and turns to step away from me. I reach out, gently grabbing his arm and pulling him to me as I enter the office and close the door behind me. "It's not about you. We are perfect."

He instantly relaxes against me, wrapping his arms around me and melting some of my nerves away. This is what I need. His arms. His touch. His encouragement, even when he doesn't know he's giving it.

"Let's sit." We sit on the small couch opposite his desk, where he likes to kick off his shoes and work in the afternoons. "Tell me what's bothering you."

I dive into a diatribe about Devante, our relationship, and all the things he did to me. I even admit to paying the asshole off to make him go away. Then I tell him the words that are going to hurt. I know because thinking them hurts me, but I have to be completely honest with the man I love.

"Ever since last night, all I can think about is 'here I go again, letting someone use me for my money.' I know it isn't true and you aren't doing that, but no matter how hard I tried, I couldn't stop the thoughts. It's been eating away at me to the point I barely slept last night." I continue by telling him about my visit with Tyson this morning. "I love you, Evan, and I'm sorry I let my past push me to a dark place, where I convinced myself you were going to do the same."

Evan is quiet for too long. He stares at the floor, out the window, at the painting on the wall, everywhere, but at me. I can see the hurt in his eyes. After minutes that start to feel like hours, he finally looks at me.

"Is that all? Are there any more secrets about you or your past that you're keeping from me?"

"No. That's it."

"Good. I don't have any other secrets, either. That means, it's time to move forward and stop letting past mistakes run our lives. We both made mistakes, but that doesn't mean we don't love each other. Relationships are about trust and communication. Now that we've finally communicated effectively, we can build a strong foundation of trust and love.

TWENTY-NINE
EVAN

 This trip is going to be great. I'm looking forward to being with our families for Thanksgiving. We flew to New Jersey late Tuesday night after Isaac's practice and spent all morning sleeping. We get to stay until Friday night, but that means taking a late flight and not getting home until after midnight. His coach wasn't happy about him missing two practices, but he allowed it so we can check on Aiden.

Since we grew up about an hour from each other, Isaac rented a large house from Tuesday to Sunday on the beach in Cape May for our families to enjoy. It's less than a four-hour drive for both families, which isn't too bad. Hopefully, Aiden won't be too uncomfortable during the ride.

I wish we had more time, but at least we get to see them, and they can enjoy the house for a couple of extra days. I think he rented the house more for Aiden than anyone else. He will be in casts for several more weeks and might need another surgery on his leg. We talked to him a few days ago and he's going stir crazy. He can't work or go to school, and other than doctors' appointments, he's been mostly confined to the house.

My parents came in yesterday afternoon and checked us into the house, bought groceries, and made sure everything was ready for everyone else to arrive. Isaac's family will be here in a few hours. Owen has to work until one then they'll make the drive to Cape May. The area is full of Victorian houses, pristine beaches, a promenade with shops and restaurants, a zoo, fishing excursions, and more. We came here once when I was a teenager and I fell in love with the area. When Isaac suggested it for our family vacation, I was on board without hesitation.

Nerves ate at me on the drive from the airport. I didn't know what to expect when I introduced my parents to Isaac. They have always supported me and even when they knew Mike wasn't right for me, they were civil to him. Mom and Isaac hit it off right away. They were laughing and joking in the kitchen as she fed my man a plate of cookies she baked while waiting for us to arrive. Dad and Isaac enjoyed a snort of bourbon on the balcony while I showered. After Isaac disappeared upstairs for his own shower, my parents let me know how much they like him. It caused my heart to soar.

The house Isaac chose is a beautiful three-story Victorian with six bedrooms and four bathrooms. We made sure our parents got the two bedrooms with private bathrooms. Aiden, Isaac, and I are sharing a bathroom and Owen and the girls are sharing one. We put them in the two bedrooms on the third floor. Isaac also made sure he found a house with an elevator so it's easily accessible for Aiden. He's in a wheelchair since the cast on his arm goes almost all the way to his shoulder keeping him from being able to use crutches.

It's after twelve when Isaac finally wakes up. I haven't been up much longer and other than saying a quick hello to my parents and grabbing a cup of coffee, I haven't been out of the room. I was still exhausted when I woke up about an hour ago, but couldn't fall back asleep, so I've been sitting in the chair by the window, enjoying the ocean view, sipping on my coffee, and reading a book. I can't remember the last time I finished a book. It's been months, maybe close to a year. Mike didn't allow such frivolousness in our relationship, and I've been too busy between work and Isaac to think about reading. The murder mystery I started when my parents were in town is sitting unfinished on my dresser.

"Good morning," Isaac's sleepy voice calls from the bed.

"Good morning." I set the book down and walk over to the bed, kissing my boyfriend. "Can I get you some coffee?" I offer.

"Yeah, thank you."

"I'll be right back. We can enjoy it on the balcony."

Mom and Dad are in the kitchen working on lunch preparations when I get downstairs.

"Is there any more coffee?" I ask.

"I made another small pot. I thought you and Isaac might need some more after getting in so late," Mom replies.

"Thank you. We are so freaking tired. Isaac's awake now, so we'll be down in a few minutes," I tell them after fixing two mugs of coffee for us.

"Lunch will be ready in about fifteen minutes, but don't rush. It will keep until you two are ready."

"Thanks, Mom. I appreciate you cooking for us. We'll be in charge of clean up."

"You will do no such thing. You are on vacation."

"So are you and you aren't going to spend your vacation taking care of all the cooking and cleaning."

"Okay," she reluctantly concedes. I give her a quick kiss on the cheek then rush upstairs.

Isaac is in the shower when I get back. I'm tempted to join him, but I feel a little awkward doing that with my parents right downstairs. Instead, I bring the coffee and a large blanket to the balcony and wait for him to join me.

"What are you reading?" Isaac's voice startles me. I didn't hear him come up behind me. "Sorry. Did I scare you?" he asks with a laugh, joining me on the small outdoor couch and pulling part of the blanket over him. It's freaking cold out here. I guess I am getting used to the heat in Miami.

"A murder mystery I found on the shelf in the bedroom. It's been a while since I read a book."

"What about the one you got when your parents were in Miami?" he asks.

"Didn't finish it." I shrug.

"And we never went to the bookstore. We'll have to do that one day soon."

"Oh, yeah, I forgot we talked about doing that. I do enjoy reading, but I never seem to find the time."

"That's because we are always so busy," Isaac deadpans.

"Don't you mean we're always *getting* busy."

"Something like that."

"Why did you stay up here reading?"

"I didn't want to leave you alone, but I felt kind of creepy staring at you."

"You didn't have to wait for me. You should have spent that time with your parents."

"I went down for a few minutes when I first woke up, but I was still really tired. I figured I'd enjoy the peace and quiet."

"Smart. It's going to be loud in here in a few hours."

"I can't wait!"

.   .   .

Isaac's family pulls into the driveway with horns blaring to announce their arrival and I love it! Growing up in a quiet, reserved home, I am surprised at how much I love the chaos that his family brings.

"Uncle Isaac! Uncle Evan!" Katie squeals, jumping into Isaac's arms then rushing over to me for a hug. Kennedy isn't as loud, but she runs to both of us for hugs. It melts my heart when Katie calls me uncle. I don't know where that came from, but I'll take it.

It takes a few minutes for Jose and Gloria to help Aiden out of the van and into his wheelchair. After he is settled inside, the rest of us unload the two cars. Katie and Kennedy take their bags and run up two flights of stairs to seek out their rooms. I've never seen two more excited kids.

Thirty minutes later, introductions have been made, cars are unloaded, and bags are unpacked. Mom and Gloria are in the kitchen with a glass of wine, discussing tomorrow's feast. Aiden is situated on one couch with his leg propped up. The rest of us are enjoying a snort of bourbon. Aiden is still taking some meds that won't allow him to drink. He's handling everything better than he was a week ago when Isaac and I talked to him. He was pretty down then but is all smiles today. Isaac was right to book this place. The change of scenery will be good for Aiden.

"What time should we plan to eat tomorrow?" Mom asks, walking into the living room with Gloria.

"Either during halftime of the first game or before the four-thirty game," Isaac responds.

Mom stares at him like she doesn't know how to respond to that. My parents aren't football fans and don't understand the importance of Thanksgiving games.

"Why don't we have it ready around two and we can watch the game while we eat," Gloria suggests.

Everyone agrees, even my parents. I guess Mom realizes she's outnumbered with this bunch.

"Who's playing in each game?" Dad asks. I appreciate him showing interest in something the Flores family loves.

"Packers/Lions at twelve-thirty, Cowboys/Giants at four-thirty and Bills/Saints at eight-thirty," Isaacs rattles off.

"It's a packed day. Can't wait to watch my Giants kick some ass," Aiden cheers.

"Ew, you're a Giants' fan?" I ask.

"Yeah, you gotta problem with that?" he asks in his best mobster voice.

"A little. Why aren't you a Dolphins' fan?"

"I am, but they aren't playing tomorrow."

"Good point. What about you, Owen? What's your team?" I ask.

"Other than the Dolphins, which we all hated until Isaac got drafted, I like the Texans by default because Dad loves them and then the Jets."

"We're all Texans and Jets fans except Aiden. It's always the youngest who's gotta make things difficult," Isaac adds.

"What can I say? Giants over Jets any day. I stick by Dad and watch the Texans, too."

I don't disagree completely. The Giants definitely have a better overall record, but I'm not a huge fan of either. I don't watch the games except for the Dolphins and if it wasn't for Isaac, I wouldn't even go to every home game.

Watching our families talk about the Thanksgiving games and witnessing how well they mesh, causes a lump to form in my throat. This is everything I need – the man I love and our families blending as if we've known one another our entire lives. If the past few hours are any indication, by the time the weekend ends, Mom and Gloria will be best friends.

THIRTY
ISAAC

"Evan," I call softly. It takes him a minute to wake up.

He blinks a few times then shoots up in the bed. "What's wrong?" he asks, panic lacing his words.

"Nothing's wrong." Isaac rubs his hand down my back, soothing me. "Come with me. I have a surprise for you."

"But it's still dark. What time is it?"

"Early. Trust me. Come on."

I stand up and walk to the closet, returning to the bed a few seconds later with a pair of thick sweatpants, a long-sleeved shirt, a pair of wool socks, and a heavy hoodie. Evan looks over my similar outfit, shrugs, and gets dressed quickly. A smile plays at his lips and I can feel his excitement. He trusts me to surprise and doesn't question me further.

As soon as he's dressed, Evan pulls on a pair of Vans. I take his hand and lead him downstairs where a small cart is waiting for us by the back door. With my free hand, I pull the cart behind me and lead us outside and down to the beach.

The air is freezing and there's a cold breeze on the beach this morning. I stop long enough to pull two wool hats out of the cart, putting one on Evan's head, making sure to cover his ears. Then I do the same with my hat.

We walk to a small alcove between two dunes. It blocks the wind but does little to help with the frigid temperature. I take a wool blanket out of the cart and arrange it on the sand.

"Sit," I command. Evan drops down onto the blanket. He's shivering, so the first thing I do is wrap a blanket around him. While Evan gets warm, I unpack a carafe of coffee, pouring two mugs and handing both to him. Then I sit next to Evan and snuggle up close, wrapping half the blanket around my body. After taking my mug of coffee, I weave my fingers with Evan's. "Watch." I motion toward the water.

In the distance, the first light of the sun begins to appear on the horizon. We sit in silence, sipping our hot coffee, hand in hand, and watch the day wake up. The sky turns from darkness to shade of pinks, oranges, and purples as the sun gets higher, peeking through clouds that are scattered across the sky. It's a beautiful sight.

"Thank you," Evan whispers, squeezing my hand.

"Before I met you, I would wake up early sometimes after a restless night and drive out to the beach to watch the sunrise. Next time, we'll do this in Miami where it isn't thirty degrees."

"I don't mind the cold. I miss it. It's a lot more fun to snuggle up to my sexy boyfriend in freezing temperatures than when we're sweating our balls off," Evan tells me.

When the sun is almost directly across from us, I take Evan's empty mug and set it on the ground with mine then cuddle closer to him, leaning in and kissing him deeply. Wrapping his arms around me, Evan pushes me down onto the blanket, propping himself up to hover over me, finally breaking the kiss.

"I love you." Pushing the beanie off, I run a hand through Evan's hair. "I need you."

"Here?" he asks with the raise of an eyebrow as a shiver runs through him.

Lust and need set every nerve on fire. I'm definitely not cold anymore and I doubt Evan is, but trying to get it up when it's this cold might be impossible.

"Probably not going to happen," I admit. Evan drops his forehead to mine.

"I've never had sex on the beach," Evan confesses, running his hand along my jawline. "It sounds fun." He glances down between us. "But you're right. It's not happening this morning. Guess we'll have to watch the sunrise when we get back home." Evan's breath hitches and his eyes widen. "That's the first time I've thought of Miami as my home, but I realize with you there that's exactly what it's become."

My heart warms at his words. Evan feels like home to me, too. "It's a date. I've never had sex on the beach, either." I kiss him again and we enjoy a few more minutes, making out on the beach as the sun gets higher in the sky. It does nothing to heat the air and eventually the cold gets to be too much, so we return to the house. I have visions of shower sex with Evan, dancing in my head. By the time we get back everyone else is awake. We greet our parents and pour ourselves another mug of coffee before going upstairs.

Owen is helping Aiden out of our shared bathroom. I know my little brother well enough to know having to have help with something as simple as a shower is driving him crazy.

"Who's next?" he asks, motioning to the bathroom when he sees us.

"Me!" Evan calls.

At the same time, I say, "Us." Aiden offers us his best gagging sound and Evan turns twenty shades of red as he rushes into the bathroom, locking the door behind him.

"Asshole," I snap, lightly punching him in the right shoulder being sure not to injure him. Owen laughs his ass off. "I'll punch you, too," I bark. Owen ignores me and helps Aiden to his bedroom.

I walk the other way down the hall to the room Evan and I are sharing. Now that I'm warm, thoughts of my wet, naked boyfriend in the shower have me fucking hard. Damn my brothers.

THIRTY-ONE

EVAN

Isaac's game is at one today, which means we will be able to get to bed early tonight. I'm exhausted after our trip to New Jersey. It was great to see our families and spend time with everyone, but we didn't get enough sleep and we both had to be at the stadium yesterday. I needed to catch up on some ordering and Isaac had a workout session and team meeting.

"Evan," Isaac calls as he emerges from his bedroom, dressed to impress in a light-blue suit. I rake my eyes over him and lick my lips. Yes, I licked my lips. My boyfriend is fucking delicious. "Like what you see?" He steps into my space, causing my breath to hitch. He knows exactly what he's doing to me.

The last week or so has been the best of our relationship. I didn't realize how much we were both letting our past relationships and secrets affect what we have. Since everything came to light, we have both been more relaxed and happier.

I clear my throat. "Did you need something?"

"Oh, I need something alright," he winks, then sobers and takes a few steps back. "Do you want to ride to the stadium together today?"

"What? Are you sure?"

"I'm positive."

"Then, yes. I'd love that. Give me five minutes and I'll be ready.

Rushing into the bedroom, I brush my teeth, pull on a pair of dark jeans, my Flores jersey, and a pair of sneakers. I put my phone and wallet in my pockets and meet Isaac back in the kitchen.

Deciding it will be fun to tease him, I say, "You know, I've been thinking. Our jobs aren't that different," I state, keeping my tone even. "Running plays, running food."

"Right," he bites out. "Getting tackled by several hundred pounds of muscle is no different than carrying a tray of chicken fingers," he continues sarcastically.

"Exactly!" I agree with fake enthusiasm as if I actually believe my words. "I have to dodge hordes of drunk people. It's a dangerous job." I rarely run food and drinks in this new position unless someone calls out, but that's not important for this conversation.

Isaac stares at me like I have three heads. He considers me for a moment. "You really believe that." It's not a question. He thinks I'm being serious.

"Of course, I believe it. Why else would we be having this conversation?"

He stares at me unblinking, trying to figure out how I can possibly believe our jobs are remotely similar or equally dangerous. The longer he stares, the harder it is for me to remain stoic and serious. He opens and closes his mouth several times, fighting for words, his beautiful, dark features a mix of confusion and amusement. I can't take it any longer. I dissolve into a fit of laughter.

"You should see your face."

"Wait. You weren't being serious?"

"No. Did you honestly believe me?"

"Well, yeah, a little," he admits with quiet embarrassment.

"A little?" I question with a raised eyebrow.

"You're kind of an evil, little man."

"Who are you calling 'little?'" I'm tall and lean, but not nearly as tall as his six and a half feet and while I enjoy working out, I'll never be a wall of muscles like Isaac. I guess in comparison, I am small.

He leans in, running one hand along my jawline. He kisses me, gently at first then deeper. After several seconds, he pulls back slightly. "Not everything about you is little," he croaks out in a deep, gravelly voice as he cups my hardening cock through my jeans. Memories of last night flood my brain. It was a good night. It was quick and dirty because we were too tired to make it last, but after not having sex for three days, we were both behaving like horny teenagers.

No matter how many times we're together, I'm ready to have him in my bed again. Or in his bed. Or on the couch. Or on the counter. Or in any number of other places we've found ourselves in the past few months. Instead, I take a step back, leaving enough space so my brain will function.

"If we don't get to the stadium, we're going to end up back in the bedroom. Can't have you worn out before the game."

"Ha, you think you can me wear me out?"

"I *know* I can."

He growls out a curse before adjusting himself. Isaac grabs his bag and tosses it over his shoulder then takes my hand and leads me to his car.

As we pull onto the highway a few minutes later, he

glances my way and speaks for the first time. "When we get home tonight, I'm holding you to your words."

"What words?" I ask innocently as if I don't remember challenging him.

Another gravelly growl escapes him before he clears his throat. "You promised to wear me out."

"Oh, yeah, I guess. I mean if you think you can handle it."

Isaac hits the steering wheel. "You're killing me. Please stop talking," he squeaks out.

I laugh softly, proud of myself for getting under his skin the same way he gets under mine. Isaac takes a few deep breaths as we make the final turn into the back parking lot where the employee entrance is located. He pulls the car into my space and puts it in park.

I start to get out, but he grabs my hand and doesn't let go. Instead, he pulls me closer as he leans toward me. His lips hit mine and for a second, I don't kiss him back. Then need takes over and I forget we are supposed to be keeping this quiet. I deepen the kiss, grabbing the back of his head and pulling him even closer.

Much too soon, he breaks the kiss, resting his forehead against mine.

"I love you. It's time for everyone to know. I'm done hiding," he whispers.

"Good. Because it's not a secret anymore," I tell him as my eye catches three smiling faces staring at us.

Some of my employees just got a show. Gossip spreads like wildfire around here. It's likely there are already pictures of us online. No one knows the great Isaac Flores, best wide receiver in Miami Dolphins history, is gay. The three sets of eyes still staring at us just struck internet gold.

EPILOGUE: EIGHT MONTHS LATER

EVAN

 I never thought this day would come. I'm sitting at my computer, paying the last payment on the final credit card. Once I hit submit, I will officially be debt free, except for my car payment. The sound of a key in the door grabs my attention. Glancing at the clock, I smile. Seven-fifteen. Isaac isn't anything if not a man of his word. He said he'd be home by seven-fifteen and here he is.

"Hey, baby! How was practice?" I ask as Isaac closes the door and tosses his keys into the bowl.

"It was good," he returns.

The first couple of months after Isaac came out last November were tough. The media ran with the story and people had a *lot* of opinions. It ate away at Isaac at first, but with support from his teammates, his family, and me, he worked through it and soon realized the opinions of a bunch of strangers don't matter.

Three days after the story broke, Mike called me. I didn't answer, but I listened to the message he left. Basically, it was almost four minutes of him groveling and begging me to call him. As the message continued, his groveling turned to anger and there was another minute of his yelling and telling me Isaac would come to his senses and leave me. He was in full rage mode when voicemail cut him off. Apparently, there is a time limit. As soon as the message ended, I erased it and blocked Mike's number. Something I should have done much sooner.

To add to the drama, Devante showed up at Isaac's the next day. He still had the gate code, so we had no warning before Isaac opened the door. I stayed out of sight while Devante threatened to go to the media and tell them everything. Isaac encouraged him to do just that. There was nothing Devante could offer them that wasn't already out or would paint Devante in a positive light. When that tactic didn't work, Devante threatened to find me and tell me about their relationship, including the money and car. Isaac again encouraged Devante to tell me everything as he opened the door wider to reveal me standing behind it. Devante was in complete and utter shock when he realized I was there. I looked him in the eye and told the manipulative asshole I already knew everything. Then I slammed the door in his face, locked it, and took my man to bed. It was a glorious day and one I will remember for a long time. Getting the best of someone like Devante gave my ego a little boost.

Isaac and I moved in together three months ago. I was reluctant when he first asked me because I didn't want to be a burden or have him feel like I was taking advantage of him. His house is paid for, and we split the other bills like electricity, gas, and groceries. He doesn't want to take money for half the bills, but there is no way I'm letting him pay my way.

How was your day?"

"Come sit and I'll show you."

He drops into the seat next to me as I remove the folder I'm using as a makeshift partition revealing two glasses and a bottle of my most expensive bourbon, one I refused to open until this moment. I pour bourbon into each glass, hand him one and take the other for myself. Then I focus on the computer in front of me.

"What's all this?" he asks.

"This," I say as I move the cursor over the word submit, clicking the button on the screen, "Is my final credit card payment. I'm officially free of credit card debt."

"What? Seriously? I'm so proud of you." He plants a quick kiss on my lips.

"There's more." I tell him, pulling back from the kiss.

"More?" he questions.

I open a new screen, showing him the excel document he created last year for me. "If I use the money I've been spending on my credit cards to pay extra on my car, I will have it paid off before Thanksgiving."

My phone dings with a text, alerting me that someone is at the gate. I press the button to let them in.

"That's fantastic! Congratulations," he says clinking his glass with mine. We each take a sip. "Damn that's smooth."

The doorbell rings and Isaac quirks an eyebrow at me, "Expecting company?" he asks.

"I'll be right back."

"Me, too, I need to grab something from the bedroom."

We head in opposite directions, meeting back in the kitchen a few minutes later. I connect my speaker and start the boy-band playlist I created for him and crank it up as his eyes meet mine.

"What's all this?" he asks, eyeing the bags of fast food.

"A celebration dinner." He's been working hard to eat better and I'm proud of his accomplishment. He hasn't stopped at a drive-thru in almost four months. "Some of your favorites. You deserve a treat."

"Damn, I love you," he says, pulling me in for a hug then handing me a wrapped gift as he steps back. "I bought this a few months ago as a congratulations for when you were able to hit submit on that last payment."

I tear into the package, revealing the eighteen-thousand-dollar bottle of bourbon I've been eyeing for the past three years.

"Oh, Isaac," I breathe out. "This is too much."

"No, it isn't. You deserve it. You've cut every corner possible and worked your ass off to budget and pay off your debt. I know this year hasn't been easy. I'm so freaking proud of you."

"Thank you."

"There's only one thing left to do to make our life perfectly complete," he tells me.

"What's that?" I ask.

He pulls out an envelope from his back pocket. "I planned to do this tonight even before I knew you were making that last payment. All the stars or whatever aligned and the timing is perfect. This is definitely a day to celebrate."

I open the envelope and read the paper, not fully catching on. It's two plane tickets to Aruba for next week and confirmation at an exclusive resort for five nights.

"How can we go on a trip weeks before preseason?"

"I talked to all the powers that be and they agreed to give me the time off for my honeymoon," Isaac tells me.

"What?" When I look up, he's on one knee with an open ring box. Inside is a simple black band. "Will you marry me?"

"Absolutely!" I cry as tears sting my eyes. I let them fall, not bothering to try to hide them. Isaac stands, pushing the ring onto my finger and then pulling me in for a passionate kiss. When he breaks the kiss and my brain catches up, I ask, "How are we going to plan a wedding in less than a week?"

"I hope you won't be mad, but I kind of already planned it. We've talked so many times about getting married and what we want, I felt confident planning it so I could surprise you. The wedding will be on North Shore Beach on Saturday morning. Simple ceremony with just our family followed by big-ass party with everyone we know. We leave Sunday morning for Aruba. If this isn't what you want, we can change it."

"Getting married at our favorite spot is perfect. How did you manage to do this without me knowing?"

"I didn't do it alone. Our mothers and Hope were a huge help. By the way, my family will arrive on Wednesday afternoon and your parents will arrive on Thursday night. I have to be at practice every day, except Friday. I took the liberty of talking to your boss and you have off starting Thursday. I have a list of a few last-minute details I'll need you... What? Why are you looking at me like that?"

"Because you are the most amazing man I've ever met. You managed to plan a surprise wedding and honeymoon. How did I have absolutely no idea? I didn't even suspect anything. I'm not sure if I should be completely impressed or horrified that you are so good at secrets," I tease.

"Impressed. I would never do anything to hurt you," he says in all seriousness.

"I know."

This man of mine is everything I've ever wanted in a partner. I'm the luckiest man in Miami, maybe the world.

ACKNOWLEDGMENTS

I would like to thank the following people for their support as I worked to complete Miami Vices. This was a labor of love and something I've wanted to do for a while. It came together easier than I imagined and that is in part to the following people.

My husband, Rick, for his constant support and love. I'm grateful for everything you have done for me over the years. You are a true partner when it comes to household responsibilities and raising our children. I appreciate you sharing this journey with me.

My children, Anders and Grady, for your love and understanding. It has been an amazing adventure and I have enjoyed every second of being your mother and watching you grow into men. Thanks you for your help and unwavering support.

My alpha and beta readers, Kim Morgan, Patty Henke, Colena Roberts, and Wendy Newell, for your feedback and advice. I appreciate your hard work and support.

Taylor Dawn at Sweet 15 Designs, LLC for this perfect cover which inspired Evan and Isaac's story.

Michelle Hoffman, at Michelle's Edits for working so hard to help me get the book finished in plenty of time.

Jess Haney and Shannon Hayes at Haney Hayes Promotion for helping promote the book.

ABOUT THE AUTHOR

Pamela Gail was raised in the rich, coastal traditions of southeast Georgia. She has been married to her husband, Rick, for over twenty years and the have two sons. As a wife and mother, she finds solitude and comfort in her creative outlets.

In addition to writing, Pamela owns two businesses that keep her busy. When she isn't working, her hobbies include reading, listening to music, wine tasting, and watching football.

To stay up to date on all things, Pamela Gail, visit her at https://linktr.ee/authorpamelagail

ALSO BY PAMELA GAIL

Where the Path Leads Series - College Romance

Path of the Heartbeats

Fixing My Path

Changing My Path

Young Adult - Standalone

Soul of Eli

M/M Romance

Better With You - Coming Fall 2023